Guns of Warbonnet

F

Guns of Warbonnet

D. B. Newton

WHEELER
CHIVERS

This Large Print edition is published by Thorndike Press, Waterville, Maine USA and by BBC Audiobooks Ltd, Bath, England.
Wheeler Publishing is an imprint of Thomson Gale, a part of The Thomson Corporation.
Wheeler is a trademark and used herein under license.

The text of this Large Print edition is unabridged.
Other aspects of the book may vary from the original edition.
Set in 16 pt. Plantin.

LIBRARY OF CONGRESS CATALOGING-IN-PUBLICATION DATA

Newton, D. B. (Dwight Bennett), 1916–
Guns of Warbonnet / by D. B. Newton.
p. cm. — (Wheeler Publishing large print westerns)
ISBN 1-59722-335-2 (lg. print : alk. paper)
I. Title. II. Series: Wheeler large print western series.
PS3527.E9178G89 2006
813'.52—dc22 2006019467

BRITISH LIBRARY CATALOGUING-IN-PUBLICATION DATA AVAILABLE

Published in 2006 in the U.S. by arrangement with Golden West Literary Agency.
Published in 2007 in the U.K. by arrangement with Golden West Literary Agency.

U.K. Hardcover: 978 1 405 63936 1 (Chivers Large Print)
U.K. Softcover: 978 1 405 63937 8 (Camden Large Print)

Printed in the United States of America on permanent paper
10 9 8 7 6 5 4 3 2 1

GUNS OF WARBONNET

Chapter One

It had been a day of changeable temper, of clouds that thinned before the autumn sun and then drew together again to let chill rain squalls march across the forest. Now, with afternoon, the ceiling had dropped until the higher ridges were lost in scudding mist. And now Ed Martin broke out his slicker, for he knew there'd be stormy weather before he could hope to get out of these hills.

He must have misjudged his distances; and it was odd. Even after eleven years, he should have remembered this Warbonnet country better. . . .

Where the trees fell back and he came momentarily onto a wide view of country ahead, he reined in the chestnut. Suddenly, through the plume of his breath, he saw movement that made him fetch up the glasses from a saddle pocket. They seemed to bring distant timber close enough to touch. But diligently as he searched, he somehow couldn't pick up, at first, the thing that had caught his attention.

Then, as he let the glasses swing in a wide arc, an open ridgeface swam into the circle of the lenses; and he held on this, for three riders were moving in single file out of the timber edge. They came at an unhurried but purposeful gait. Two wore slickers — the third, a plaid mackinaw. He couldn't make out faces, but he saw the stock of a saddle gun thrust from below one bent knee. The riders crossed the clearing and were gone again. And he lowered the binoculars, frowning narrowly.

For all you could tell, there might be an army combing these timbered sweeps.

But then he shook his head. This didn't necessarily mean anything. After all, it was the changeover of the season, a time when ranch crews would normally be searching the hills for stock overlooked in the move down to winter range. Ed Martin said aloud, gruffly, "There'll be trouble where you're going, all right — but don't go finding it where it isn't!"

He put away the glasses in a sour mood, and urged the chestnut gelding ahead down this stock trail that should, eventually, take him to the valley floor. For perhaps the hundredth time, he asked himself if he couldn't somehow have ducked this assignment.

Hendryx, his boss, had apologized for putting the pressure on him; and yet, the pressure had been strong enough. "If I had more men, and more time," he'd said, "I could let you off. But it looks like things are building to a blowup. I need someone who knows that Warbonnet country and won't have to waste time floundering around, trying to get the feel of things."

At least Martin had given him an argument: "It's eleven years or more since I left. And even supposing one man could do any good, staving off a fence war — it's not a matter for us. Any man's free to put wire on land he owns, or holds under lease. No federal laws have been broken that I know of."

"Not yet, maybe. But the tip we have about Mort Browder shows how the wind is blowing. Browder's only the first. Let a full-scale range war get going and we'll see every kind of hired gun and outlaw flocking in there — the same ones that have been raising hell up in Wyoming. We can't let the Warbonnet become another Johnson County."

Which made sense, all right, even if he

was reluctant to admit it.

Now, as he rode, the rain started — no more at first than a quiet sibilance high among pine branches. Daylight dimmed as successive layers of mist wrapped these hills away from the sun; chill of the autumn storm began to cut through the folds of his slicker. Ed Martin kept tracking over that scene in Hendryx's office:

". . . I don't have to warn you about Browder. You'll have plenty on your hands if you do cross trails with him. And yet, he's actually little more than a pretext for me to be sending a man in there. What I really want to learn is, how close things seem to an open break. I want to know who Browder's 'connection' is — if he was really sent for, and if any other gunfighters are being hired. On either side."

"What about the local sheriff — will he cooperate? This Burl Adamson is new, since my time."

"You'll simply have to feel him out. There's a chance he may be glad to get some help, at a time like this. On the other hand, some of these county lawmen can get mighty touchy over any sign of interference from federal officers. You'll have to handle him with gloves, till you see which it's going to be. In fact, no part of this job is going to be easy — I want you to know I realize that."

"Thanks!"

It wasn't a hell of a lot of help. . . .

And yet, he had to admit he'd often thought about someday making his return to the Warbonnet. There were questions that needed to be settled, before he could close out that chapter of his life. Like finding out if Owen St. Clair still held him to blame for Hal's death — in particular, seeing if the years had fulfilled the promise of Eve St. Clair's beauty, or done anything to dim his old feeling for her. Of course, he wouldn't have wanted to come back with his tail between his legs, the way he'd left. But maybe this way wasn't much better — riding in with authority that would almost certainly put him in the opposite camp, and widen even further the breach with the St. Clair family that had once been the very center of his existence. . . .

When a single gunshot suddenly broke across the hills, shrouding rain muffled the echoes so that it was hard to judge the source at once. Somewhere fairly close, Martin thought, his head jerking up and his hand yanking the damp reins involuntarily; somewhere to the south of him. He couldn't ignore it. As soon as he decided there was to be no second shot, he pulled his horse in that direction and used the hooks.

The ground lifted to a low, curtaining ridge where pine trunks were black and streaked with moisture. He went up across the toe of the ridge, dropped into the draw that lay beyond; and as he did, a roan with an empty saddle came through a belt of timber and halted, uncertainly, on catching sight of him.

Martin rode down, and seeing that the horse was about to bolt he spurred quickly in, heading it. Pine needles gouted under steel but before the animal could take a new direction he had reached and grabbed its headstall. He saw the brand — a Rafter 9, a new one since his time. "So-o!" he said, gently, to settle the frightened animal, and leading it went on down into the draw. As he rode he unhooked the fastenings of his slicker and pulled the skirt of it back, leaving clear the Remington that he wore against his leg, in a low-cut holster.

Where this draw emptied, the land leveled out in a narrow park belted by pines; and here a man lay motionless. At a glance, Martin knew he was dead.

He had that definite look of death. The sight of him stiffened Ed Martin in the saddle and made his hand tighten on his gun, and half lift it from the holster. But then he let the breath out of him with a grunt, and allowed the Remington to slide back into leather. Afterward he rode out of the timber, still leading the roan. Dismounting he dropped reins and came to a stand beside the body, with no expression at all showing on his dark-skinned, sharp-boned features.

The man was a stranger to him. He had been a few years older than Martin, in his middle thirties perhaps. He must have died instantly; he lay face down, in the loose, grotesque sprawl of a violent ending — arms thrown wide and head twisted and one leg bent up under him, at an unlikely angle.

Martin considered him for a long moment; then, with the revulsion for death that a man never quite overcame, even when he'd had to become well acquainted with it, he went down on one knee and took the man by a shoulder to turn him over. The bullet had got him in the chest and his plaid shirt and denim jacket were dark with blood. The head rolled limply, dead eyes staring. An arm flopped over — and something fell from the half-curled fingers.

Ed Martin stared, and felt the sudden quickening of his pulse as he reached and picked the object from the damp needle litter. It was a six-gun shell, .45 caliber. It was still warm, and a trace of pungent powder-smoke swirled inside the blackened brass tube.

He took a deep breath, and his mouth set hard. He tossed the cartridge, catching it in his hard palm, and dropped it into a jeans pocket. He straightened to his feet, then — and in the next moment he was turning, quickly, as riders broke out of the trees at the lower end of the park.

They saw the dead man and one of the pair cried, "What the hell! It's Bill Hammer!" His eyes swung to the stranger. His mouth pulled down. Without warning a spurred heel kicked savagely; the horse under him shuddered and lunged straight forward.

Ed Martin was seconds slow in leaping aside. The animal pounded by him, earth trembling to the irons and the heavy, muscled shoulder barely missing him. His own chestnut, and the dead man's roan, split apart and scattered before the charge; one of them trumpeted shrilly. The rider was already pulling up, yanking his horse about for another wild try at running the stranger down. Martin saw the rage that twisted his face, the gleam of the gun that leaped into his hand.

As he pawed at the skirt of his slicker, he

heard his own voice yelling something. Then the bronc plummeted at him again and his boot slipped on slick grass and pineneedle litter. At the same moment, and without warning, the weight of the second rider dropped full upon his shoulders and bore him to the ground.

He felt the gun bounce from his holster. A knee rammed solid muscle at the back of his thigh — a crippling blow. But though he landed underneath, he lit rolling, and the material of his slicker pulled free of the grappling hands. He got away, and managed to come up to his knees and get one boot set under him. Then he held where he was.

The one who had tried to run him down was leaning from saddle, holding a naked Colt trained at his head. He gritted savagely, "Watch what you do, killer!"

Chapter Two

There was no arguing with a drawn weapon. Ed Martin held himself carefully still. The rider turned, lifted his gun, and deliberately punched a pattern of three shots, evenly spaced, toward the low clouds: echoes of the signal rolled away through the mist.

Rain had started falling harder.

Martin climbed to his feet, wincing a little at the pain of the leg that had been kneed. He who had fired stepped down from the saddle, now, holding his gun steady on the prisoner with blue smoke dribbling from its muzzle. A smell of wet rubber began to rise from the slickers of all three men.

The second puncher had got his breath back, after making that wild tackle. The hair that he revealed when he dragged off his hat and ran a hand across his forehead was blond, pale enough to look bleached. He replaced the hat, and pulled his angry stare away from the stranger. He turned and walked over for a closer look at the body on the wet ground; and now he knelt to unsheath the dead man's revolver.

"It was only the one shot we heard, all right," he told his companion, nodding bleakly. "Bill's gun ain't been fired."

"Nor mine, either," Martin cut in. "If you don't believe me, go take a look at it! You think I killed this man," he went on, when the pair merely eyed him. "I want to prove to you I couldn't have."

The punchers exchanged a coldly unbelieving look, but then the blond one shrugged and went over for Martin's Remington. He picked it up from where it had fallen, glanced at the loads; Martin saw the sudden puzzlement that pulled at the corners of his long mouth. He sniffed the barrel, and lifted his eyes to his companion, in bewilderment.

"By God, it's the truth! This gun ain't been fired!"

"The hell you say! Lemme look!" The first puncher took it from him, made his own examination. He scowled and scuffed a palm across a heavy mustache, as he lifted a stare at the stranger. "All right! If you didn't do this, then who did? And where did he go?"

Martin answered impatiently, "There was no one in sight when I got here. I can't tell you any more than I know!" He added, "If you want to catch the murderer, you'd better be looking for sign before this rain washes it out!"

"Reckon we'll wait for Mr. Casement," the man with the mustache said flatly. But he told the blond rider, "See what you can pick up."

"Right," the latter agreed, and rode out of the clearing, bending from saddle to search the ground as he went.

"Who's the dead man?" Ed Martin asked.

"Our boss," the other answered shortly. "Bill Hammer — foreman of Rafter 9. Dammit to hell, he was riding with us — not half an hour ago. . . .”

Suddenly more horsemen were breaking out of the trees — summoned, apparently, by the signal of the pistol shots. There were two men in slickers, a third who seemed to have come unprepared for the rain and instead wore his red mackinaw's collar turned up. That coat identified the trio for Martin; they were the same ones he'd seen through his glasses, earlier.

One of them, riding a big, blocky dun, seemed the leader; he gave an impression of strength, within the shapeless folds of his slicker. A fairly handsome man, Martin thought, though his face appeared to be marred by a constant and truculent scowl. As he drew rein he was saying, “You find something, Flint?”

And then he saw the body sprawled on the ground and Martin watched him stiffen, seeming to grow taller in the leather.

Flint, the dark-mustached man whose gun still covered Martin, said, “Somebody killed him dead, Mr. Casement. Whitey and me heard the shot, and we found this hombre here with the body — but it looks like our first guess was wrong: Don't appear he could have done the shooting. So I've got Whitey hunting for sign.”

Casement's look had come to settle on the stranger. Dark eyes, in the too-intent face, studied him. "My name's Casement. I own Rafter 9 — and Bill Hammer was my foreman. Now, suppose you tell us who the hell *you* are, and what you're doing here!"

Martin had started a hand toward the gap of his slicker, but he held the move as Flint's six-gun lifted dangerously. He looked at the gun, and at Casement. "I came over the pass," he said coldly. "As for who I am — there's something in my coat pocket, if you'll give me a chance to get it out."

The rancher exchanged a look with his man. "*You* get it," Casement told Flint shortly. Martin waited as the slicker was pawed aside and a hand roughly searched his pocket. A look of surprise warped the puncher's face; he brought out what he had found and scowled at it. "Arch, the guy's a lawman! This here's a deputy U.S. marshal's badge!"

"What!" Flint handed it up. Arch Casement took and studied it closely, and again put his eyes on the stranger.

"You damned sure this is yours?"

Martin only looked at him, as though the question wasn't worthy of an answer.

The man in the mackinaw had kneed his bronc forward. "Lemme see!" As he reached to take the badge, the heavy coat fell open. For the first time, Martin caught the dull gleam of a sheriff's star pinned to the shirt beneath.

So this would be the Burl Adamson he was supposed to make connections with and, if possible, work with. Martin looked at him more closely, and with immediate misgivings.

He saw a paunchy individual, who looked uncomfortable in the saddle. His florid, close-shaven face ran to jowls, making sagging brackets on either side of a petulant mouth. Right now the sheriff's lips were blue from the chill. Scowling, he looked at Martin and he demanded, "Who sent you here? Why was it done without consulting me? *I'm* the law on Warbonnet — and I didn't ask for no federal men!"

Measuring the man, Martin tried to keep the dislike from showing in his voice. "Looks like you've got one, anyway," he said, and saw the sheriff's scowl deepen.

"You haven't told us your name," Casement now reminded him bluntly. But there was no time just then for an answer; the blond puncher they called Whitey was spurring back, suddenly, bending to fend aside low-hanging pine boughs. He was orey-eyed with excitement.

"Boss! I've found his sign! He waited for Bill under the trees yonder. After the killing, he headed north." The slicker rattled as the fellow swung an arm, pointing.

Casement barely glanced in the indicated direction. He nodded curtly. "All right."

"But there's something more, Mr. Casement! The bronc he's forking has got a twisted frog on the left rear shoe!"

"Then it has to be the same man!" the puncher named Flint exclaimed. "It's the one we been chasing all afternoon, Chief — the same that slaughtered St. Clair's beef! Bill must have got too close and he turned on him!"

Whitey added, "That's how I figure. Two reasons, now, we got to nail him! But we better be moving!"

"All right — all right!" Casement cut him off with a gesture. "All in good time! I'm not through here, yet." Ed Martin had been looking at Casement at the moment Whitey made his revelation, and he was still puzzled to put a name to the expression he'd seen. Not surprise, exactly; not quite shock, either. More like a sudden, nearly uncontrollable rage.

But the expression was fleeting. The man's eyes were empty as he turned again to the stranger. "You were about to give us a name. . . .”

Martin shrugged. “A name by itself doesn’t mean much,” he said. “But here’s somebody coming who should be able to identify me.” And he nodded past Casement and the sheriff.

Four new riders were just now entering the clearing. Like the Rafter 9 men, they were all in slickers or ponchos, all with hats pulled low against the misting chill. The damp hides of their horses set up a fine steam; each mount bore a Chain Link brand.

Heading the group was Owen St. Clair, his rail-lean figure stiffly erect, on a good-looking black gelding.

The years had changed St. Clair but little. His face, hawkish and fine-seamed, was beaten to a mahogany color by a lifetime of bucking tough country. His hair, that swept in wings above his ears and hung almost to his shoulders, was the startling clean white that yellow bleaches out to when it ages. Fierce blue eyes, under shaggy brows, scowled at the group, peering through the whispering needles of rain. A braided leather riding crop dangled from one gaunt wrist.

“Somebody fired the signal,” he said. “What is it? What have you found?” And then he saw the body that still lay on the ground, and his eyes widened. "Bill Hammer! What's happened to him?"

"He's dead," Casement told the old man. "Murdered. We figure he caught up with your stock killer, and didn't get to a gun in time."

The old man showed visible shock. "This is hard to believe!" he exclaimed. "Cutting a fence is one thing. Maybe, even slaughtering a dozen head of beef. But to do it to a man — that don't hardly sound like Tom Sheridan, or any of his crowd! It don't hardly sound like what a sane man would do!"

"Whitey Lewis found tracks," Casement said impatiently. "They prove it was the same did both jobs." Then, as the other continued to shake his head in scowling puzzlement, he made a gesture toward Ed Martin. "Take a look at this man. He says you should know him. Ever seen him before?"

Martin stood waiting, as the weathered head turned in his direction. Heavylidded eyes settled on his face, and held there a long moment, blank and devoid of recognition. But then, slowly, it dawned. Martin saw it light the steely eyes with an unbelieving, furious glow, and saw the thin mouth draw down into a harsh line. The hands holding the reins clenched so tight that the knuckles stood out like bony knobs.

"You!" the old man exclaimed, and his voice shook.

"That's right, Owen," Ed Martin said quietly. "It's been a long time."

"I never thought you'd have the nerve to come around here again!"

Martin drew a long breath. This was turning out no better than he had always been afraid it would. "Eleven years is a long time to carry a grudge," he pointed out, and waited through a silence that was broken by the jingling of a bit chain as one of the horses tossed its head, made restless by the fine stinging of the rain.

"A federal marshall now, I heard somewhere." St. Clair snorted in contempt. "I ain't impressed. I know the truth. I know you never had any good in you!"

"The fact remains," Martin said, "I've been sent here to do a job — not to rehash personal differences."

"Then do your job — whatever it is. Just see that you keep out of *my* way. Steer clear away from Chain Link." The hooded eyes snapped with a malignant fire. "And especially from Eve!"

Martin felt his cheeks stiffen, a mask for the boiling of hard emotions. Anger made him say crisply, "That last, I won't promise. It would have to be up to her!"

"By God!" The riding crop lifted, clutched in a trembling hand. "I used a horsewhip on you the last time I saw you. I can do it again!"

Martin knew he should hold his tongue, but he heard himself saying, "I wouldn't put it past you to try! Apparently you haven't changed at all. Except you're a little more arrogant, more opinionated —"

There was a tremulous shout from the old man and the riding crop came down. The first blow, striking the side of Martin's head, sent his hat tumbling; he felt as though the ear had been torn away. Eyes blazing, St. Clair lifted the riding crop a second time but Martin's arm, upflung, broke the weight of the blow. He stumbled back from it. The old man called him a vile name as he kneed his horse, trying to crowd nearer and inflict punishment on this man.

Then, belatedly, Sheriff Adamson recovered presence of mind. He had been gasping like a fish, staring at this eruption of violence. Suddenly he kicked his mount with the spurs and, ramming in, grabbed St. Clair's horse by the cheek strap and pulled him away. "Here — here!" he cried. "What's going on?"

It was Arch Casement who answered him, as the old man let himself be hauled from his intended victim. "You've been around awhile. Surely you've heard the story of what happened to St. Clair's son, up at Gold Camp eleven years ago."

The lawman's eyes widened as it hit him. "You don't mean — ? This ain't the one that — ?"

"He's quite right," St. Clair told him, breathing hard. "This is Ed Martin — that took my boy up there and got him murdered!"

"That's not quite the way it happened," Martin said, gingerly touching his hurt ear. He knew protest was futile, and he spoke without heat; despite the whipping, he had himself under better control now.

"You can't deny you caused his death — as sure as if you'd pulled the trigger yourself!"

"I denied it plenty, eleven years ago, but my denial made no impression on you then and I guess it doesn't now." He raised his shoulder in a shrug, inside the wet slicker. He was smitten with self-disgust, suddenly, for letting himself be goaded into quarreling with an old man who'd once been the same as a father to him. "Whoever's got my gun," he said, "I'll take it now."

The man named Flint looked at his boss and Casement nodded shortly. Face expressionless, the puncher reversed ends and handed over the Remington by its barrel, and Martin slid it into holster. "Here's this," Arch Casement added, and flipped the marshal his badge, spinning it off a thumbnail. Martin caught it from the air, started to drop it into his pocket; then deliberately, he pinned it to the front of his shirt instead.

Casement waited until he was finished, wearing that hooded scowl. He said coldly, "And now let me make a suggestion. I don't know what business you think you've got here in Warbonnet, but I do know you've caused this man and his family enough grief already. You've been told that you're to stay away from Eve St. Clair. If her father's direct order won't stop you — maybe mine will!"

Martin looked at him sharply. "Yours? And what have you got to do with it?"

"It happens that Miss St. Clair and I are engaged to be married."

Martin blinked. Eve St. Clair — and this scowling, unfriendly man? He was handsome enough, in a way; and Ed Martin had told himself all along that he must be prepared to return and find Eve had been married. But unless the years had made her far different from the sunny, warmhearted girl he remembered, there was something about this particular pairing that struck him as very wrong. . . .

But no time now to ponder it. Arch Casement was turning to his men, saying bruskly, "We've fooled around here too long already. Gentry!" He spoke to the man who had ridden up with him and the sheriff. "Help Bud Flint get Hammer across his saddle, and I'll let one of you take him back down to the ranch." He looked coldly at Ed Martin. "You're welcome to go with them, in case you've forgotten the trail."

"Thanks," Martin answered curtly. "I'm not lost." He turned away to his horse.

There was a busy moment there in the clearing, as Flint and the other puncher picked up the dead foreman and hoisted him face down across his rain-wet saddle, using his own rope to lash him in place. Ed Martin had remounted. He saw Gentry eyeing him, obviously waiting, the reins of the lead horse in his hand. "Maybe I don't make myself clear," the marshal said to Casement. "I'm riding with the rest of you."

"The hell you are!" the sheriff snapped. "This is a local matter — some small-fry ranchers that have been making trouble by cutting fences and killing stock. Now it looks like they may have turned to murder. A federal badge doesn't give you authority to shove your nose in!"

"I'm afraid you're wrong," Martin answered. "Since you've been wondering what I'm doing here, I'll tell you. . . . Any of you heard of Mort Browder?"

They went still. "Browder?" the sheriff echoed. "Who *ain't* heard of him?"

"That madman!" cried St. Clair. "What would he be doing in Warbonnet? Just months ago, he was involved in that Johnson County trouble, in Wyoming."

"True enough. He dropped out of sight, after that. We tracked him to the Hole-in-the-Wall and from there he disappeared; occasionally we'd run across a trace of him, but always too late. Then, a couple weeks ago, the marshal's office in Denver had a tip that indicated Browder was headed for the Warbonnet."

Arch Casement's eyes narrowed. "Are you suggesting it was Browder killed my foreman? You'll have to show me proof!"

"Maybe I can. Maybe you've heard that Browder has his own way of earmarking his killings? In Johnson County, a dozen men were found where he dropped them — and in each victim's hand was the shell of the bullet he'd been shot with." As they stared at him Martin lifted his hand, a spent cartridge between thumb and forefinger. "When I came across your man, just now, this was lying in his palm. Still warm!"

It was St. Clair who exclaimed, "You don't make sense! Why would he advertize himself — maybe even bring the law down on him? It isn't reasonable!"

Martin shook his head. "Browder's not a reasonable man. He's half insane, by all accounts — a murderer for hire, at so much per head, and completely jealous about claiming credit for the killings he contracts to do."

"And you're saying someone's brought this monster in here? That he's being paid to slaughter our beef and commit murder?"

The sheriff exploded. "Hell! Anybody can put a shell in a dead man's hand! For that matter, how do we even know you found it there? This could be nothing more than ruse, so as to let you horn in on a local matter!"

That was a close hit, Martin thought, looking at Burl Adamson in some surprise. Aloud he said, "Sure — it *could* be a trick. But there's nothing you can do but take my word that it isn't!" He pocketed the shell, picked up the reins. "Right now the trail's getting colder — and wetter. And there's not much daylight left." He jerked his head at Whitey. "Come on. Let's have a look at that sign you found, *I'm* interested, if nobody else is!"

The blond puncher hesitated, casting a glance at his boss. Casement was scowling but he appeared to have nothing to say; so Whitey shrugged and reined after Martin, who was already spurring into the trees.

Once, before the rain-dark tree trunks came between, Martin looked back and saw Gentry disappearing by the downward trail, Bill Hammer's limp body swaying facedown across the back of the lead horse. The rest of the group were coming in the wake of Martin and the blond puncher. There was leashed anger in their faces — but they were coming.

Chapter Three

The rain continued — icy where it struck against a man's face, occasionally even laced with pellets of sleet. The higher they climbed, the lower the clouds lay upon the timbered upthrusts surrounding them. Mist clung and drifted in tendrils among the tree trunks, as gradually the dimming light was filtered out of the day.

Sheriff Adamson was the one who finally called quits. A thinblooded man, he had been having a miserable time of it; his face was blue with chill and his heavy body shook in spite of the plaid mackinaw. Ed Martin felt no surprise when he suddenly hauled rein and said, in an irritable voice, "Why are we kidding ourselves? We're going on guesswork! There's been no sign at all, the last couple of miles — and in another hour it's going to be dark."

Owen St. Clair gave him a cold stare. "You suggesting we should turn back?"

Under his glance the lawman wavered. Martin had already gathered he didn't have much love for manhunts, being the kind of officer who preferred to administer the law from behind a desk. He seemed to wither now under St. Clair's open scorn, while his hands holding the reins shook uncontrollably. But, surprisingly enough, Arch Casement came to his support.

"I'm inclined to agree," Casement said. "I've kept hoping we could figure the man out and decide just where the hell he was headed. Now I don't know. It's not the pass, obviously; and he doesn't appear to be trying to circle back toward the low country again, either. I think it's plain we've lost him."

Martin, looking around at the hunched shapes of the riders in their bulky slickers, with the mist of congealed breath hanging before their faces, saw in all of them except old St. Clair this same inclination to accept defeat. Later, he would remember feeling that Casement's willingness to give up so easily contrasted oddly with his look of shock and fury on learning his foreman had been murdered. But at the moment, Martin was too angry himself to pay much attention. He said impatiently, "One thing certain, in weather like this our man's bound to head for cover. I've been wondering: Is there anything at all left up there at Gold Camp?"

It was a touchy thing, he knew, to bring that subject up again in St. Clair's presence. Cold hatred was in the hooded eyes the old man turned on him. "Not a hell of a lot," St. Clair answered. "Time you took Hal there and got him murdered, it was still a producing camp. Since then the mine's shut down and the place is emptied out."

"Still, there must be *something.* Buildings — places where a man can hole up. . . ."

Casement shrugged. "That fellow Riley's still around. He's caretaker for the mining company, keeps a supply of liquor he sells the punchers or anyone else who happens to wander over that way."

"You know, it's a thought, though," St. Clair conceded, frowning over it. "I wouldn't put anything past a man like Riley. He certainly wouldn't hesitate to harbor a killer. . . . It might be worth a look."

Martin, seeing the determination in the old man's gray, pinched features, had to grant him real respect. Evidently he was too tough still to admit that a day of mountain trailing and weather might be too much for a man of his years and brittle bones.

The sheriff looked unhappy. "I never been to this camp," he said dubiously. "How much farther is it?"

"Another hour's hard riding at least," Arch Casement answered; and when he saw the misery in the sheriff's raddled cheeks, St. Clair's mouth took on an open sneer.

"Looks like it's just too much for the sheriff. Well, he's free to fall out any time he feels like it."

Adamson's eyes bugged. He opened his mouth wide. "But I never — I only said —"

"There's enough of us here to handle any killer," St. Clair broke in curtly. "After all, if we should need the law —" and his wicked glance flicked at Ed Martin. "— we've got a federal marshal with us. So, you go on home, Mr. Adamson. You'd probably only hold us back!"

Obviously the sheriff had put his foot in, that time; and he knew it. At the arrogant dismissal his chilled features changed color and became oddly mottled. He tried one last protest but St. Clair had already turned away. And Adamson let the protest die. Staring at the old man's back, he looked positively sick.

The incident and the look were enough to warn Ed Martin that local politics here remained as they had always been. Despite his years, Owen St. Clair must still be the big man on the Warbonnet; by earning his scorn the sheriff had let himself in for bad trouble. In all likelihood he could measure the end of his days in office from this moment.

But though Martin felt embarrassment and even a little pity at the lawman's disgrace, it was nothing for him to interfere in. He kicked his own tired mount, falling in as the riders moved off in a new direction. They left the sheriff sitting in the saddle, motionless, his mackinaw a dim red blur against the dark, rain-streaked masses of the pines.

Black night covered Gold Camp, wrapping it in mist and muffling every sound. The eight horsemen took a slippery trail down off a low rim and turned into what had been the camp's one street, past the dark sprawl of a reduction shed and the mine buildings and the scattered shacks that were now decaying and lifeless. A single lighted window was the only faint gleam of brightness. Overhead a man could almost feel the pressure of the low cloud ceiling.

They rode slowly, and when St. Clair spoke and halted his horse the rest pulled in to hear what he had to say. "Riley and that woman of his are a couple of shady characters," he told them. "I've had trouble with them before. If they know anything, they wouldn't tell us; but maybe we can put the fear of the Lord into them."

The building that housed the single light — a peaked-roof hotel-and-saloon combination which had been almost the only two-storied structure in camp — rose directly before them, dimly visible against the darker timber and the black sky. The window was steamed over; it let a muted glimmer of light fall upon a decaying veranda and broad, sagging steps.

The riders dismounted in a clump of trees and tied. The rain looked as though it could be over, though it might start again. Ragged clouds were streaming overhead in the wind, scraping the ridge. A few stars showed intermittently. Not wanting to be hampered, Ed Martin stripped out of his slicker, folded it and strapped it behind his cantle. He indicated the dark bulk of a barn that stood behind the hotel. "I'm going to have a look at what's inside there."

There was no comment, but when he started for there both Arch Casement and Owen St. Clair fell in beside him — whether this was because they considered his idea a good one, or simply to keep close check on any move he made, was an unanswered question. Inside the dark structure they heard the stirring of horses in their stalls. As Martin let the door swing shut behind them, Casement popped a match on his thumbnail and held it high. A barn lantern hung from its nail driven into a roof prop and he took this down and got the wick burning.

The barn was a small one, with a hay mow, a dozen stalls flanking a center aisle, and another door at the far end. There was a smell of moldy hay. Five of the stalls were occupied; Martin heard St. Clair's exclamation and saw that he was staring at a bay with a Box S branded on its shoulder. "That's Tom Sheridan's saddle horse!" He looked squarely at the lawman. "And, you, and your Mort Browder! What have you got to say now?"

Martin shrugged. "This isn't the horse we've been trailing."

There were two others in the forward stalls, one of them also bearing the Sheridan brand, the third unmarked. Ed Martin gave a single searching glance, and then was moving down the straw-littered aisle to the far end. There, at his approach, an ugly-looking sorrel tossed its head and its eyes shone back the lantern glow. He caught the Snaketrack brand on its shoulder, turned sharply to say, "Here we are! Bring that light back here!"

Shadows wavered and swung as the pair came to his summons, the swaying circle of light reaching about them. Martin pointed to the Snaketrack. "That's a Wyoming brand," he said. He dropped to his knee, then, tapped a rear leg until the horse finally grunted and shifted its weight off it. And motioning the light closer, he picked the hoof from the floor and showed these men the worn shoe, and the twisted frog.

A long run of breath, like a sigh, broke from Owen St. Clair. Martin, setting the hoof down, got back to his feet. "Well," he said. "Now we know."

"Maybe," Arch Casement conceded dubiously. “At least it looks like we’ve found our murderer.” He pointed to the saddle and blanket, both still damp, that were racked on the stall partition. “We’re in luck.”

“Unless he’s already spotted us,” Martin said. “If he has, he can give us the slip the same as he did in the Hole-in-the-Wall!” He slid the Remington from its holster and looked at the loads, his thoughts ranging ahead in the businesslike way of a man who knew his job and was preparing now to go into action. “As a precaution, I’d suggest we post a man here at the barn, another with our own cavvy of horses. And, don’t forget — the man we’re up against has already killed today. He’s going to be dangerous to handle.”

“All right, all right!” St. Clair answered shortly. “Let’s get at it.”

Casement turned and was starting back along the aisle when Martin warned sharply, “Blow the lantern before you open the door. . . .” They sent Whitey to watch the barn, detailed one of St. Clair’s riders to guard their horses and be ready if things should get out of hand. That settled, the remaining six men tramped across the spongy mud to the hotel entrance.

There had been no sound from within, nothing to hint their quiet arrival had been detected. A live wire of tension pulsed in Ed Martin, and he let his gunhand rest on the butt of the holstered Remington. Warped porch boards, lying loose on rotted stringers, rumbled a sudden dull thunder under the concerted strike of boots. Then Casement's hand fell on the latch, and a shove of Casement's meaty shoulder threw the door wide. They entered as one man.

Things had changed sadly since the night when Hal St. Clair met his death here. Even then — in the last days of Gold Camp's wild boom — Martin supposed it had been tawdry enough, though a kid of eighteen was not too apt to realize that. Now, whatever it might have had once was gone.

The big wagon-wheel chandelier was missing, and its reflectored kerosene lamps. Gone were the sparkling backbar mirror, the gaming tables and the roulette layout and the Wheel-of-Fortune, the noisy mining crowd, and the crimson velvet tassels on the stairway leading up to regions that had seemed tempting and exciting. Now this room was no more than a cavernous place of shadows, lit by a single smoky lamp on the bar, and by the glow of the fire roaring behind the isinglassed door of the space heater sitting in a box of cinders. There was scarcely even any furniture left — a few chairs, a couple of squat round tables. That was all.

No one in the room could possibly be Mort Browder.

At one of the tables, three men in range clothing and sheepskins were at work finishing up a meal; as the newcomers burst in, bringing the chill of the night to set the flame dancing in the lamp chimney, they craned around in their chairs. A fork rang against the table edge, clattered to the floor, and one of the men came lunging to his feet in a clumsy scramble that sent his chair crashing.

Ed Martin had recognized only one of the three — Tom Sheridan, owner of Box S. He hadn't changed a lot. The lines were worn perhaps a little deeper around his mouth, the dark and bushy hair was peppered now with scatterings of gray. He sat where he was, level eyes in an intelligent and sober face watching the newcomers approach.

Over at the bar the proprietor, a fellow named Joe Riley, had been leaning on his elbows. He straightened now — a seedy-looking man who had once been a dandy, with a ruby stickpin glowing redly in his cravat. Now he wore an old waistcoat, spotted with grease and frayed at the pockets, and a soiled candy-striped shirt buttoned at the throat but with no collar. Strands of thinning black hair were combed in a saddle across the naked dome of his head.

He looked at the newcomers and then toward the men at the table. Riley would know all these men of Warbonnet, know the cross-currents of interest that had set one rancher against another. His expression was that of one who sees destruction threatening to break loose on top of him. He managed speech.

"Mr. Casement . . . St. Clair! This is more people than I've seen here in one day, in a long time. Storm must be sending everybody to cover. . . ."

He got no answer from anyone. The door slammed shut and in a dangerous silence the newcomers deployed themselves; Bud Flint and the two Chain Link riders, needing no orders, posted themselves back in the shadows near the entrance, where they could cover the room if necessary and the darkened stairs. Their bosses moved directly toward the bar and the table.

Joe Riley cleared his throat and tried again: "Hope this rain's been enough to do Warbonnet some good. But, I guess, when a range goes gaunt it takes a lot to bring it back. . . . Hazel!" he yelled across his shoulder, adding, "If you gents are hungry, we'll be glad to fix you up with something."

It occurred to Ed Martin that he had eaten nothing since a fairly skimpy breakfast of trail rations. But no one else was thinking of food. Owen St. Clair said flatly, "It's not what we're here for!"

His tone stilled the proprietor's scared chatter. Riley swallowed and now his hands were trembling; they tightened on the edge of the bar. Owen St. Clair said sharply, "Who owns the sorrel?"

"What sorrel, Mr. St. Clair?"

"The one in your barn — branded with a Snaketrack." The old man turned to the table. "He belong to one of you, maybe?"

They exchanged a look. Besides Sheridan, there was a young fellow with the look of an ordinary puncher; the third, who had leaped to his feet when the door opened, was short of stature and stockily built — about forty, with sandy hair and beard, and a nose that had been broken and spread flat across his face. One eye had a squint and a milky cast to it, and gave the impression that it must have been blinded in the same mishap that smashed his nose for him. He stood with legs braced, and there was naked hatred in his voice as he shouted, "Any good reason we should tell you anything?"

Tom Sheridan, still seated, lifted a hand

and touched his companion's elbow, shaking his head. "They've got six to our three," he said calmly. "Seems like a good enough reason. . . . No, Owen," he went on, his look meeting St. Clair's. "None of us rode a sorrel up here. Snaketrack's not even a Warbonnet brand."

The old man studied him and his companions, for a long moment. Then he swung to the man behind the bar. "Riley?"

Riley shook his head. "I don't know any such animal."

"The hell you don't! He's out there right now — eating a bait of your oats and hay!"

"By God, let me take a look!" Riley turned and started to round the end of the bar.

A word from Casement halted him. "Stay where you are! Flint, see to it he does!" There was a small movement, over in the shadows by the door, and Bud Flint's six-gun was out of its holster and leveled on the proprietor, who blanched and halted with his shoulders pressed against the back-bar. "Nobody moves from here," Casement said, "until we learn what we want to know, if we have to search the building and the whole damned camp!"

"I don't suppose," Tom Sheridan said, "there's any chance of you telling us what you think you expect to find?"

"We might — after you tell us what the three of you happen to be doing here."

The one who looked like a puncher said heavily, "That's none of your Goddamned business!"

Two swift strides carried Arch Casement to the man, rounding the table and kicking a chair out of his path. His arm traveled a short, hard arc; there was the splat of fist striking flesh and the puncher was knocked from his chair and sent sprawling.

Ed Martin had been holding back, waiting to learn how St. Clair and Casement meant to handle things. Now he had seen enough. "Stop this!" he said crisply and moved forward.

Not turning, still standing over the man he'd felled, the big man said again, "Flint!"

The voice from the shadows said, "It's all right, Chief. I got the marshal covered."

Martin jerked around. Bud Flint was eyeing him and the gun was trained squarely on his chest. Martin's cheeks tightened with fury. "You don't know it, Casement, but you're on the verge of making a bad mistake!"

Now Casement turned, slowly, and a cold stare settled on the marshal. "You're a long way from Denver, Martin," he said lightly. "And the fact that my foreman was murdered means a hell of a lot more to me, just now, than any tin badge you happen to wear on your shirt! So, let's say you take that gun out of your holster and lay it on the bar!"

Martin stared. He had met arrogance before, but never such utter contempt for the office he represented. Obviously this Arch Casement — this scowling man to whom Eve St. Clair was supposed to be engaged — was an enigma, and a tough and ruthless one. Martin swung his glance toward St. Clair, thinking perhaps here he might find some trace of sanity; but old resentments had blinded the Chain Link owner. Martin's jaw hardened, and his own impotence to stop what was happening roiled high in him. Without a word he walked over to the counter and laid his Remington on the wood, next to the lamp that gave this room what light it had.

Flint said warningly, "Now, move away from it." And with the puncher's gun trained on him, he complied. The heat of the lamp beat upward into his face as he turned to see what Arch Casement thought he was going to do next.

The one Casement had felled was getting to his feet again, clutching at a chair to help pull him up. A dribble of blood leaked from a corner of his lip and he touched a sleeve to it, gingerly. And now, slowly, Tom Sheridan pushed back his own chair and rose, to face Casement. He had the grave look of a man suddenly realizing the seriousness of the situation that confronted him.

He said, "There's no need to get tough with Ollie Rayburn! You know he just rides for me — he only does what I tell him."

"Then tell him to keep his fat mouth shut!" Casement warned. "And all three of you — shuck your guns and toss them out here in front of me."

"Like hell!" cried the man with the broken nose. But the protest died in his throat as he saw more than one six-shooter drawn and leveled on him. The trio of prisoners exchanged a long look that was fraught with apprehension. But they were helpless to resist; slowly Tom Sheridan took his weapon from the holster and tossed it to the floor, and a moment later those of the other two thudded after it.

"That's better," Arch Casement said; he let the muzzle of his own Colt sag a little, but didn't holster it. "Now let's hear the answer to some questions. How does it happen the three of you are in Gold Camp, the same day we chase Bill Hammer's murderer here?"

Sheridan said, in a level and steady voice,

"I give you my oath! This very minute is the first we knew about anyone being murdered. For the past two days we've been over at Cassville. We came across the pass, this afternoon, and got caught in the storm. That's the whole truth!"

"And what would you be doing in Cassville?" old St. Clair demanded.

"If it's any of your business," the man with the mangled face answered him, "we were trying to get rid of some stock. Shape it's in, after this past summer, we've got precious little that's fit to market; and none of the outfits on our side of your damned drift fence have grass enough to hold them another winter."

Sheridan took it up quickly, plainly trying to head his companion off from hotter argument. "Luke Frazee, here, thought he knew some feedlot men who might take a few head off our hands, and at least give us something for them. We rode over to find out."

St. Clair said sharply, "You sure you didn't go to meet a crazy gunslinger named Mort Browder?"

Sheridan's eyes slowly widened. *"Browder!"*

"You heard me!" All at once St. Clair was shouting, head thrust forward on his turkey neck. "You sure you didn't arrange with him to report to you here — after he'd had time to look over the ground and maybe commit some deviltry? Like, slaughtering beef and doing a murder or two?"

Tom Sheridan had drawn himself stiffly erect. "It's not true, Owen! You've known us too long to make a charge like that!" His face, Martin could see, was deathly pale beneath its weathering.

Luke Frazee, he of the battered features, looked on the accuser with a gleam of pure hatred in his one good eye. "You got a hell of a nerve, old man," he gritted. "That sounds more like the kind of thing a man would do who'd fence cattle away from water and grass — at a time when a whole range was in trouble!"

"Meaning me, I suppose?" St. Clair shouted back. "Or, maybe you're claiming Arch Casement hired someone to kill his own foreman!"

The puncher, Ollie Rayburn, was still daubing at his cut lip; he glowered above a bloodied fist, at the man who had hit him. "Me, I wouldn't put even that past him — if it'd get him anything! Casement's stopped at nothing else since he come here and started trying to take over this country. I dunno how he got *you* under his thumb the way he has. . . ."

Sheridan made a frowning gesture, to silence his man; but the damage was done. For Ed Martin, looking at Casement, saw the fury in his eyes and saw Casement's hand tightening on his gun. Suddenly, he had a premonition of what was about to happen.

There was no time to reach Casement, no time to try to stop him. But the oil lamp stood at Martin's elbow. It was an unplanned and nearly instinctive move that swept his arm against it, and sent it crashing to the floor.

Chapter Four

The glass chimney splintered; the big room was engulfed in darkness except for a dancing glimmer of fire in the iron-bellied stove. But an instant later the darkness was torn apart by muzzle flash as a gun roared, deafeningly. Someone cried out, a second shot smashed on the heels of the first.

Martin's vision was blurred by afterimage, as he sought blindly across the polished counter for his own Remington. His fingers located it, pushed it away, found it again; quickly he grabbed it up.

Hoarse voices were yelling excitedly in the

big room. Boots were trampling; a table crashed over.

More shots, then, the purple flashes crossing each other and the concussion enough to lift the top of a man's head. Martin crouched against the bar with the burnt-powder stench in his nostrils and his gun gripped tight, but useless — a man must be a fool, to work a trigger in this indiscriminate darkness. He shouted Casement's name but got no answer. Again a weapon sounded off and he heard a slug hit the big stove with a clang like a blacksmith's hammer. Behind the bar, Joe Riley was mumbling shakily under his breath — praying, maybe.

Bud Flint shouted suddenly, "Boss! Look out — the window!"

Pivoting that way Martin saw a blocky shape and an upraised chair; the man — it was Luke Frazee, he thought, the one with the disfigured face — swung, and glass and frame gave with a splintering smash. A second blow sent the piece of furniture crashing bodily through what was left of the window, and then the man followed it in a headlong dive that seemed completely reckless of the drop to the hard ground below.

It was Flint's gun, over near the door, that drove a bullet after the fugitive. Martin gave a curse and pushed away from the bar. Arch Casement's voice shouted, "Stop them, Flint! We want them all!" Even as he spoke, Casement turned and collided blindly with Martin, a shocking impact that drove a surprised gust of breath from the big man and halted them both for an instant. Ed Martin didn't hesitate. His gun arm lifted and fell, and real anger was in the weight that he put behind it. He felt the barrel strike home, though the blow was cushioned by the crown of a hat. The weapon slid away, glancing off the point of a blocky shoulder. And Casement collapsed, rubber slicker rattling as he fell directly at Martin's feet. The latter had to catch himself to keep from stumbling over him.

Across the room, at that instant, the door wrenched open and someone went charging through. Martin went after him, at a run. Someone grabbed for him in the dark but he shook off the hand and heard St. Clair's exclamation. A gun sounded, outside, and then a second time. Martin lunged through the door and the cold outer air breathed against him.

Somewhere to his left, he thought, Bud Flint must be hunting the man who'd escaped through the smashed window. With wind pummeling the pinetree heads just south of the hotel and whistling around the eaves, it was difficult to make out anything for certain. As he stood there on the porch, unsure of his next move, a weapon exploded under the trees and a bullet struck the building front, a yard from him.

That would be St. Clair's man guarding the cavvy. Damned fool, he thought — not even knowing what he was shooting at! Martin dropped prone onto the loose boards of the porch and a perverse impulse drove him to steady his wrist against the flooring and punch a return shot, aiming high because he didn't want to risk hitting the horses. He rolled on across the edge of the porch and dropped lightly to the ground, where he waited at a crouch, hearing the bunched animals stirring in their fright. But at least that other gun kept silent.

Then, over in the barn, a horse trumpeted shrilly.

It took him an instant to realize what that sound might mean. But when it came again, together with a striking of shod hoofs against timbers, the truth hit him like an explosion.

On the thought, he had his feet under him and was moving at a run across the softened earth, raising the freshening smell of the rain with every step. Tattered clouds rode the higher winds; there was no moon, but the immense stars of this high country laid down a frosty glimmer of their own. It showed him the crumpled figure lying motionless at the corner of the barn, just before he would have stumbled over it.

Gun in hand, Martin knelt to make hasty examination. As he turned him over the fellow groaned; so he wasn't dead. The hat fell away from his head and Martin saw dimly the light thatch of blond hair it revealed. This was the man called Whitey; and Whitey was the one who had been left to watch the barn. A single glance at him brought Martin to his feet again.

His hand was on the door, ready to yank it open, when he heard a sound at the back of the barn and knew it was too late. He let the door bang shut and turned quickly, running now along the face of the building to the corner. He came to a stand again beside Whitey's faintly stirring form, and saw the horseman bursting from that other door at the rear.

At first he was hardly more than a formless shadow, bent low to clear the doorway; but then he straightened in the saddle and Martin had a momentary glimpse, at least, of a spare shape, strangely thickened at the shoulders, and of a pale hint of a face turned in his direction. He had never seen the legendary Mort Browder, but something told him beyond any doubt that this must be he. The surprise of it held him an instant too long. Then he remembered his gun in his hand and he lifted it.

But Browder was already merging with the shadows. He lowered the gun, unfired.

Within seconds more, Ed Martin was among the tie-up of horses, under the trees. No time to look for his own mount; he took the first at hand, ripped loose the knot in the reins and rose quickly to the saddle. As he did, the guard suddenly appeared at his stirrup, pawing at his leg and yelling startled questions. Martin simply booted him aside. He backed the horse free and gave it the steel.

The gunfight inside the big building seemed to have ended. Someone came slamming out onto the porch to yell at him as he went by. Ignoring him, Martin set his borrowed mount straight up the throat of the gulch.

He could guess at Browder's probable actions this evening. He'd have expected no pursuit as far as Gold Camp. He'd ridden in and put his exhausted sorrel in the barn where it could get a feed, but then he'd stayed out of sight; probably getting wind of the presence of strangers, he hadn't wanted to let himself be seen by Tom Sheridan and his companions. The coming of a second group of riders would have made Gold Camp too crowded for a man like Browder. When the shooting started, distracting Whitey's attention, Browder had had a chance to jump the guard, get his Snake-track horse from the barn and escape.

Rain-slickened mud offered treacherous footing, and the borrowed mount nearly floundered to its knees a time or two. Martin lifted him with the spurs, and with a firm hand on the reins. Shortly, they were above the main bulk of the camp's buildings, and here he pulled up for a moment, testing the darkness.

The night seemed full of sound — the blowing of the animal between his knees, the rushing of wind and drip of moisture in the brush. Below him, he could hear an occasional shout from the excited men hunting among the buildings, and once a gunshot sounded, as someone thought he saw a target. Martin turned his attention toward the black wall of the mountain rising directly before him. Overhead the clouds were breaking up more rapidly, now, running before the wind and letting the starlight through. It showed Martin the dark shapes of the closed-down mine workings, directly ahead — ancient tailings heaps, and scattered buildings. To his left was the odd, sprawling outline of a reduction shed, lying at a steep angle up the mountain's face.

It was no definite sound or other real clue that told him to look for Browder there; but when he turned the horse in that direction he became aware, almost at once, of a prickling of the short hairs at the back of his neck. It was an altogether eerie feeling, that he ascribed to the weird flow of half-light and shadow, and the noisy night that lay around him. Partly, too, to an uneasy awareness of the quality of the man he was stalking through this wild darkness — a killer who, he was convinced, must be more than a little mad. . . . He could feel the muscles across his shoulders bunched painfully tight. As he reached the near corner of the long shed, he reined in and shifted his shoulders to ease them.

Above him, toward the upward end of the long, sprawling building, a gun lashed purple flame; the slap of the report was almost swallowed by other sounds. Taut nerves leaped and caused the horse under Martin to toss its head, as it felt the jerk of the reins. But then a trained reflex brought Martin's gun whipping up, and the Remington bucked against his palm. He fired twice, then slammed barbed heels against the horse's flanks. It leaped forward, and fell into a buckjumping climb that fought the steep pitch of the slope, carrying him quickly higher along the slanting side of the reduction shed.

Martin expected he would be riding straight into another bullet, and braced himself; but no second shot greeted him. He thought instead he heard a flurry of hoofsound, wasn't sure. Seconds later he reached the upward end of the building and pulled in again, close against the corner of the decaying building. Gun ready, he searched for any sight of his man but somehow knew that Mort Browder had already left this area behind.

He held where he was, as he tested his memory. He had been here only once before in his life — eleven years ago, when a couple of eighteen-year-old lads had ridden up to Riley's, drawn by rumor of delights forbidden and only half guessed at; one of those boys had never ridden away again. Martin's knowledge of the place was scanty enough, but he tried to picture this upward end of the camp. There would be a trail from the head of the gulch, he felt sure; and if Mort Browder had scouted the layout — as he undoubtedly would have — then he would know his escape route. The conviction grew on Martin that he was hunting an enemy already gone beyond his reach.

He kicked the horse and moved ahead, through the remaining clutter of decaying shacks that looked at him with eyeless windows partly boarded over. Brush scraped his stirrup fenders. Then this fell away suddenly and he pulled up, wondering if the open where he stood could be the remnants of a trail. The thought brought him out of the saddle, pouching his gun as he dug for sulphur matches. He went down to a hunker as he popped one alight on a thumbnail. The wet wind promptly blew it out for him. He swore, and shielded the second one between his palms as he played its flickering light over the ground, looking for old wagon ruts or — if he was lucky enough — fresh hoofsign.

He saw neither. He hadn't fairly begun his search, when a yell lifted to him from the downward slope; and then riders were climbing toward him, coming fast. Martin dropped the match and straightened quickly, as a voice beat up at him: "Who's there? Hold steady, while we have a look at you!"

It was the voice of Owen St. Clair. He

sighed and called back, directing his answer at the high shape of the old rancher that was clearly limned now in the starlight: "This is Ed Martin. If it was anybody else, I could have knocked you off your saddle by this time!"

He stood and let them come up to him, in a storm of hoofbeats. As they pulled rein, horses blowing and stomping and saddle leather creaking, St. Clair demanded, "What are you up to?"

"What would you think?" Martin retorted. "I was after Browder, but he got away from me. Maybe you can tell me if there's a trail leading out of this gulch?"

"I wouldn't know," St. Clair answered shortly. "I ain't familiar with this place and I don't want to be!" And one of the Chain Link punchers added, "He's probably good and gone by this time. No use looking for him in the night."

This sounded wholly reasonable, and Martin admitted as much. "It will have to wait till morning, I guess," he said. "Unless Joe Riley has a better idea."

He was turning to remount his borrowed horse, when a word from the old man halted him. "No so fast, Martin!" Looking around, he saw starlight glimmering off the six-gun that St. Clair was holding, its barrel slanting squarely down at him. "Take his gun!" St. Clair ordered his men.

"What is this?" Martin demanded sharply.

Without answer, the three punchers with St. Clair swung down from their saddles, and one of them — a slabby, blunt-featured man he'd heard the others call by the name of Harry Doyle — reached for the Remington in the lawman's holster. Martin started to protest, but there were too many of them; he let the weapon be plucked from his holster, and flung aside into the brush. Martin looked up at the old man, still in saddle, and said again, "What is this anyway?"

"Ed Martin," the old man told him curtly, "it's my opinion you stand in need of a lesson. I warned you once already — I don't want you here; but that doesn't seem to have made an impression. Maybe you don't think I meant what I said."

"I think you meant it, all right," Martin said. "I'm sorry you feel this way. I bear no grudge, over what happened a dozen years ago; I'd be pretty small if I did, considering all I owe you. And maybe I can understand you holding me responsible for what was done to Hal. But your feelings aren't going to stop me from doing what I was sent here to do!"

He could all but feel the sharp old eyes bearing at him in the dim light. "And what of my daughter?"

Martin shrugged. "Eve's a grown woman — and the best judge of what she wants and doesn't want. If what she wants is a man like Arch Casement, that's her business. But if she has no objections to me looking her up while I'm here — then nothing you can do is going to stop me!"

"You think not?" Saddle leather creaked as the old man shifted position. "Looks like I was right," he said heavily. "You need a lesson!" He must have made some sort of signal, then, that Martin didn't catch; for, at a step, two of St. Clair's men moved in on either side of him and suddenly his arms were seized and clamped tightly. He swore and twisted, trying to tear loose, but they had caught him by surprise and he was a prisoner before he knew it. And now Harry Doyle stepped in, and took Martin by the front of his coat and pulled him up. The man's other fist made a short, arcing swing and stars danced across Martin's vision as knuckles struck him in the face, solidly.

No words were said; in a deadly silence, Doyle went about his task while St. Clair sat watching and the other pair held Martin for the heavy fists to work on him. It didn't take long. Unable to defend himself, Martin couldn't stand up to such punishment. He tried to pull his head back, to ride with the blows, but soon he was too groggy. The hat fell from his head. When a smashing fist struck the ribs above the heart, he felt as though it had crashed on through. His legs buckled and one of those who held him prisoner lost the grip on his arm and let him go down onto his knees. He tried to catch himself and found his hands pawing at someone's leg. Hard leather and cold metal were under his fingers. With his last rebellious strength he closed them on the butt of a holstered gun and, crouching there, pulled the weapon out and tried to swing it around on his tormentors.

Someone shouted, "Watch the gun!" And with a curse, Doyle moved in and the sharp toe of a boot struck Martin's wrist, a painful blow that came near to splintering the bone. He grunted in pain as his fingers flew open and the gun went spinning out of his grasp.

As though from a great distance, Owen St. Clair's voice came to him through the cottony plug that seemed to be swelling inside his head: "That's enough! Let it go, Harry! Don't want to hurt him permanent."

Doyle muttered something. Whether he

didn't hear the order, or chose to ignore it so as to get in a final lick to end this business his own way, Martin never knew. But next moment he took a blow squarely in the face, that completed what had been nearly finished already. His head was flung back on his neck so that he stared straight up at a sky full of ragged clouds, and lamps that were stars. And then someone turned the lamps down.

They went out entirely. He didn't even know when he was dropped and left to lie, face down, on the damp earth.

Chapter Five

A cloying scent made its way into his consciousness, past the barrier of dull, aching pain. He lay testing it, wondering about it and trying to decide, without opening his eyes, just where he was. As awareness grew, the scent seemed to grow stronger. It was woman-smell — perfume — but too intense to be really pleasant. It seemed to impregnate the bedclothes pulled up close about him, the pillow under his head. But there was another odor behind it, too — something indefinable, something like the smell of decay. . . .

He opened his eyes — one of them; the other seemed swollen shut. Light stabbed at his vision and made him squint and try to turn from it. He was looking directly at a window; the shade had been pulled but it was an ancient one and the green fabric was scored by a network of cracks through which sunlight poured in a dazzle. He turned his head, then, and saw the woman.

She was in a rocking chair beside the bed; she had gone asleep sitting there, and her head had fallen forward so that he couldn't see her face. Her hair looked drab and colorless. She had on a man's shapeless coat, against the chill of the room, and her feet were shoved into worn carpet slippers. Yet Martin knew somehow that the perfume was associated with her.

The wall behind her had been papered, at some time or other, with a design of huge red and yellow roses; but the paper was stained and peeling and gave off the sour odor of decay he had noticed behind the overlying, cloying sweetness. The room itself held scanty furnishings that were scarred and sadlooking remnants of better days, like the wall paper. The bed was clumsy, iron-framed. There was a bureau, a couple of chairs, a clothes press with a sagging door. On the bureau an oil lamp — useless, now that morning light had taken over — had burnt down and was sending a pungent tongue of black smoke curling up the throat of the glass chimney. Martin cleared his throat. He spoke into the stillness.

"That lamp is starting to smoke."

The woman woke with a start, lifting her head. She wasn't young, though the raddled memory of spent beauty still managed somehow to cling to her; now, her eyes were swollen with sleep and her faded hair had come undone, and the coat she clutched about her for warmth hid whatever was left of her figure. She blinked at Martin for a moment, as though only partially wakened. He had to repeat his statement before she looked around and then got up, went to the bureau and blew the lamp. She made a face. "God! What a stink!" She went to the window then, ran up the shade and forced open the warped sash. Fresh, pine-sweet morning air began to flood the room. The sun was well up; he could see it, above the granite ridges.

He knew by now where he was — somewhere in Joe Riley's establishment, likely in a second-floor bedroom. He said, "How did I get here?"

Standing at the foot of the bed, the woman looked at him. "You don't know? You don't remember walking down the gulch?"

"All I remember is falling on my face, after Chain Link got through with me!"

"Well, you must have had some spit left — enough to get you on your feet. We started wondering, when you didn't show up after the ruckus in the bar. It was quite a while after the others left, that Riley heard you stumbling around, clear out of your head. What did they do to you, anyway?"

He shrugged, tentatively putting a hand to his face; his fingers found tender spots and an eye that felt like an immense bruise. He was relieved to find that his nose didn't seem to have been broken by the Chain Link puncher's punishing fists. His body was so sore that even raising an arm was enough to make him wince.

"You must have done some work on me," he said.

"Only washed off the blood," she said briefly. "Wasn't much else to be done."

"I remember you!" he said, suddenly. He had been studying her face, trying to bring a nagging recollection to the light. "Eleven years ago, but I'm sure I remember. I'm trying to think of your name. It was — That's right! Hazel something-or-other."

"It was Hazel Riley," she said nodding. "It still is. We just never advertised the fact Riley and me were married — seemed better for business." She added, "And so you knew my name! You must have a pretty long memory!"

Martin grinned a little. "Maybe it's just that you made a big impression!" he said, and saw how the compliment heightened her color with pleasure and seemed to take away some of the years that had put their stamp on her. "After all, I wasn't much more than a kid. I'd heard plenty about Riley's, but I didn't have any real idea what to expect. I walked into that big room, that night, with the chandeliers and the red velvet and the roulette tables. I heard the music, and saw what looked to me like the half-dozen most beautiful women I'd ever laid eyes on. But your face was the one that stuck. . . ."

Tired eyes softened slightly; with an unconscious gesture the woman raised an arm in the old coat and touched her bedraggled hair. "I wasn't bad," she admitted, "if I do say so myself! But there's been a lot of changes since those days," she added, and her eyes dulled again. She glanced at him appraisingly. "You've changed, some, too."

"You remember me? And, that night?"

"I wouldn't be apt to forget it!" Her

mouth twisted. "It was the beginning of the end for us, here at Gold Camp. If Riley'd known who you were — if he'd known the kid with you was St. Clair's youngster — he'd never of let the pair of you light. He never should have, anyway! I could see you both was green as they come — that's why I sort of took you under my wing, personal, not wanting some of them chippies I had working for me to get their claws into you. And then those drunks started their fight — and young St. Clair took the bullet that wasn't meant for him. . . ."

Ed Martin said bleakly, "Hal St. Clair was my best friend — a little wild, but a hell of a good kid in spite of everything the old man could do to spoil him."

"I gather that his pa still blames you for him being here that night. As I got it, the whole thing was the other boy's idea."

Martin shrugged. "It was his idea — but I didn't argue very hard against it! All the things we'd heard about Riley's, it sounded mighty exciting to a young fellow with a wolf he'd never had a chance to cut loose, down at home in Warbonnet.

"As for the old man," he went on, seriously, "I figure it's understandable, the way he felt. He knew my background. I was nothing but a range orphan — my ma a laundress at an army post, my pa a horse-breaker who made a living gentling remount stock for the cavalry. Owen St. Clair practically took me in out of a snowdrift and raised me, right along with his own son and daughter. Why shouldn't he take it for granted I was the one who led his boy astray?"

The woman tossed her head. "If you want to make apologies for the old bastard, that's your affair. *You're* the one he horsewhipped and kicked off the place!"

"He's changed," Martin insisted. "He didn't use to be the way he was last night — mean and ornery and vindictive. I loved him like he was my own pa. I guess maybe the years, and the troubles down on the Warbonnet, have soured him."

"I wouldn't know about that," she said. "Riley and me ain't apt to waste any sympathy on him. He tried his damnedest to close us down, afterwards; he even tried to raise a vigilante mob, to ride up here and burn us out. Then, a year or so later, the mine shut down and the camp died, and we about died with it.

"They hired Riley to stay on as a watchman, to guard the property. I wanted him to move on, but I couldn't get him to. I wore myself out fighting it. And so —" She made the gesture with one gaunt hand, that included the scrubby furnishings of the room, the decaying building, the camp lying dead around them. Abruptly, then, she shrugged and dismissed the topic. "You're lying there starving while I talk your arm off! Let me fetch you something to eat."

"No!" Martin pushed himself up, setting his jaw against the protest of a battered body. "I could eat, all right. But I won't have anybody waiting on me!" Then, as the covers fell back, he grabbed them hurriedly. "Hey! Where are my clothes?"

She looked at him with amusement. "Now, don't go getting embarrassed! It's only your shirt — I took it off you so as to spot the blood out of it. Here, it's dry." She took the garment from the foot of the bedstead and tossed it to him. "If you're not too stove up, come on downstairs. I'll have something for you."

"Thanks," he said. He felt the bristles on his jaw. "I'd like to shave, too. If you can find a razor."

"With your face cut up like that?" She shrugged. "Well — it's your face. . . ."

Alone, he eased himself to a sitting position on the edge of the bed and wasn't able to hold back the groan that broke past his clenched teeth. He sat a moment probing the bruised flesh above his ribs. None broken, he decided; nothing worse with him than bruises and a cut face. Moving carefully, he shrugged into the shirt, and then hooked his boots one by one with a bare foot and hauled them to him. He worked into them and then got gingerly to his feet.

. . . The big main room downstairs was even more tawdry by daylight. The stair carpet was worn through on nearly every tread; the balustrade, that he kept a hand on as he made his way carefully down, had a couple of spokes missing. The window, smashed in the fighting last night, was the final touch — a gaping hole in the wall. Joe Riley, out on the veranda, was at work now with hammer and boards, closing it with a makeshift shutter that would at least keep out the weather, and much of the room's light as well.

Martin sat at the same table Sheridan and the others had used last night, and ate the breakfast Hazel Riley brought him — warmed-over potatoes fried in bacon grease, cold biscuits, black coffee. She poured herself a cup of the strong stuff but let it get cold, as she sat across the table from him in moody silence, listening to her husband banging away. The man came inside as Martin was finishing up; he dropped the hammer on the bar and ran a hand across his thin saddle of black hair, shaking his head as he surveyed his handiwork. "That looks like hell!" he said glumly. "Guess I'm gonna have to get me some glass up here and build me a new window."

"Sure!" his wife said, in weary sarcasm. "I know when *that* will be! Things fall apart a little worse every day. They never get fixed."

"Well, can I help it?" Riley lashed back. There was an air of defeat about this place, and these people — living here in the dead remains of Gold Camp's tawdry past, and with no future to look forward to.

Done with his sorry meal, Martin turned to ask the man, "What finally happened last night, after I lost out?"

The man and the woman exchanged a look. Riley lifted his shoulders inside the grease-spotted waistcoat. "It was a mess, all around! After Luke Frazee busted the window, Tom Sheridan and that redheaded puncher of his managed to get out through the kitchen. Hazel says the cowboy was shot — I don't know how bad."

"I saw some blood on him," his wife said in answer to Martin's questioning look. "And Sheridan was holding him up. While the rest were hunting Frazee, they got a chance to reach their horses in the barn and sneak out."

"And Frazee?"

"He got away — so far as we know."

Martin frowned and scrubbed a fist across his jaw, feeling the sting of the marks of Harry Doyle's mauling fists, aggravated now by the work he'd done with Riley's long-shanked razor. Impatience beat high in him. "I better be trailing," he muttered. "That is, if I still got a horse. You didn't see anything of a chestnut gelding running loose — Hourglass brand on him?"

"He's in the barn," the man said grudgingly. "I figured he must be yours. I gave him some grain."

"Good enough!" He got to his feet, the chair scraping the ancient floorboards. He reached in a pocket. "What do I owe you for the breakfast?"

The woman started to say, "We wouldn't think of asking —" but her husband cut in, stabbing a look at her. "That'll be a buck," Riley said gruffly. "We got to eat, too!"

Martin brought out a couple of silver dollars, dropped them on the table. "That'll cover the grain for the horse," he said in a dry tone. "And one more thing, while I'm at it. You heard the name of Mort Browder, last night. You said you didn't know anything about him."

Riley scowled, weak-looking eyes blinking. "I know the name. Ain't he the killer them Wyoming cattle barons hired, last year, to clean out the nesters for them up Johnson County way?"

Martin nodded curtly. "The same. He's not only a killer, but from all reports he's more than a little crazy — nobody at all you want to monkey with, take my word for it." He paused. "He was in your barn last night; I chased him out after he buffaloed that white-headed rider of Casement's. You're still sure you can't tell me how he got there?"

"I don't know nothin'!" Riley said gruffly. "And I don't take sides in what's going on down on the Warbonnet, either. It's nothing to me if St. Clair and that fellow Casement have went and strung barb wire across what grass the drought ain't finished off; though I reckon Sheridan and the rest are ready to go to war to get it down.

"The old man caught Luke Frazee, one time, using a pair of wire cutters, and he gave him a good one with that riding crop he always carries. Broke his nose and damaged his eye. I understand St. Clair offered to pay for a doctor; but I reckon Frazee would sure enough kill him if he ever had the chance."

"I reckon," Hazel Riley said, and Martin nodded in understanding. This should explain the vindictive hatred Martin had seen in Luke Frazee's battered face, whenever his one good eye lighted on Owen St. Clair.

"Well," Riley said, "maybe one of those people would go so far as to bring in professional talent — maybe they wouldn't. I don't know 'em well enough to judge. Less I do know about the goings on down there, the less chance I have of getting involved in something that's none of my put-in!"

Martin considered this argument for a long moment; then he nodded, again. "All right," he said. "Just so you understand what you're doing. . . ."

He was in the barn, saddling the chestnut and strapping the bedroll in place behind the cantle — and pleased to find his belongings all intact — when the woman came to him. She stood in the chill of the barn interior, rubbing a work-roughened hand over her arm inside the shapeless coat, a scowl on her face. She said abruptly, "Riley lied to you, about that Browder fellow."

"I figured so," Martin agreed, as he continued working.

"At least, I *think* he was lying. . . . What's this man look like?"

"I've never seen him. There's a police picture, though, on file down in Denver. Thin-faced man — pale-eyed. . . ."

"The man I'm thinking of had the strangest face I ever saw on a man. So narrow you could have almost sliced steaks with it. Eyes that looked more dead than alive."

He nodded, grimly. "You've described him! Go on. When did you see Browder?"

"It was five, six days ago. He rode in over the pass; or at least I figured — he never said. He never gave out any information at all, but he asked plenty. He had a way of pumping you dry — with those eyes looking at you, you kept talking whether you wanted to or not! He wanted to know the whole setup on the Warbonnet, and I reckon Riley gave him an earful. He was here about three hours. Had a couple of drinks and something to eat. Then he rode on."

"And did you see him again yesterday?"

"No, I had no idea he was back. He must have kept out of sight. I don't know how his horse got in the barn without us finding out."

Martin considered what she had told him. He asked then, "That day Browder was asking for information, did he ask about anyone in particular? Did he mention names?"

"Not that I know of. Why would he? The

man's a stranger."

He shrugged. "The Denver office had a tip we consider reliable, that Browder was boasting about an opportunity of some kind he had waiting for him in Warbonnet. That's why I'm here. We want to stop the war that's building, if it's physically possible."

"You're saying, you figure someone's hired Browder and brought him here — one side or the other. Is that it?"

"About the size of it."

"And you're going in there alone, after him?" The woman gave him a long appraisal. "I dunno. Guess you realize you ain't likely to have a single friend. Whoever handed you this job ought to have his head examined. Or, if you volunteered — *you're* the one that needs it!"

"You don't hear me arguing!" he said bleakly. He turned the stirrup for his boot and swung astride. "Thanks again for everything," he told the woman. "If Browder should show up a second time — watch your step with him."

She shrugged. "Nothing's going to happen to me. Nothing ever does!"

When Ed Martin rode out of the barn, ducking to clear the doorway, the woman stood looking after him — a woman embittered and hardened by life. It had been a tough life, maybe even a sordid one; but at least she didn't plead for mercy, now that she'd fallen on bad times. You had to grant her that.

And it was something to know he appeared to have at least one friend here. . . .

Chapter Six

He found the place where he'd taken the beating last night, identifying it by the many boot marks in the mud. His hat lay there, trampled and sodden. He punched some shape into it, and afterward searched the brush and discovered his Remington a half dozen yards away, where Harry Doyle had flung it. Martin wiped the weapon dry, checked the action, and just to play safe replaced all the shells with fresh ones from his belt. Then he sent his chestnut up the slant into the narrow gulch, trying to pick up Mort Browder's sign again that he'd lost the night before.

It was a raw morning, despite the sunlight. There was a pummeling, blustering wind that whipped from every part of the compass, tore at his clothing and pushed him about in the saddle; it was like the voice of the mountains, talking of more bad weather ahead with the near onset of winter. Martin found the sign he was looking for, and it led him up into the timber across the ridge behind Gold Camp; twice he discovered the clear and unmistakable prints of a shoe with a twisted frog. But with a trail that many hours old he couldn't expect his luck to last. The sign too quickly played out, and all his searching failed to turn it up again.

After all, Mort Browder had had plenty of time by now to get down out of these hills. If he was still hiding here, then to go poking about blindly hunting for him could be the surest way to invite a bullet between the shoulders. After last night, Browder would likely be on his guard and as mean as a prodded rattler.

Meanwhile, an anxiety was growing in Martin to know what might be happening down below, down in the Basin. Yesterday had seen blood spilled on Warbonnet. One man was murdered; and at least one other — Ollie Rayburn, that puncher of Sheridan's — had been wounded in the shooting scrape at Gold Camp. There was no certainty things had stopped there. In a situation this tense, it could have been enough to touch off a powder train and start the very holocaust he was here to prevent.

It was this sense of urgency that turned

him back, abandoning a trail it seemed useless to try to follow any longer and setting his course downward again out of these hills and close-packed timber, toward the open rangeland. But he didn't like to admit his feeling of real relief when the last of those handy ambush sites fell away, and the ache of tension eased from the spot between his shoulders.

Ed Martin was only moderately fast with a gun, himself. In the course of carrying a deputy marshal's badge he had been shot at many times and had killed his share of men. He didn't know how well he could expect to stack up against a man like Mort Browder, though he was willing to take his chances if his job called for it and he could do it face to face: but it was the thought of an enemy skulking in the timber — out of sight and able at any moment to take a leisurely bead on him — that could make the cold sweat start beneath the brim of a man's hat. . . .

Broken clouds streamed before the wind. The sun was nearly overhead when he came out of a shallow draw and the Warbonnet stretched before him, open and inviting, between a sheltering southern ridge and the scarp of a grassy plateau to the north. After a summer of continuing drought, the valley floor looked seared and gaunted. It didn't take a man as long familiar with this range as Ed Martin to recognize the signs or to know that they would mean serious trouble for the men who lived here.

As the basin floor began to level out, he came upon the river itself — shrunken by drought until it was shallower than he'd ever seen it. It paralleled his course for some distance, far below and between steep walls it had carved for itself. He rode on into the heart of the basin, and the land became increasingly familiar.

Once he pulled up at a place he especially well remembered, where a tumble of timbered granite broke the river's course. Below this island the divided waters came together again, in a quiet pool where he'd often sunk a hook and line and always pulled out a good mess of trout. An ancient deer trail had given access to the river, a hundred feet or more under the rim where he sat; but when he looked for this he saw that at some time in these eleven years, a slide of rocks had obliterated part of the narrow shelving. He paused a long moment, looking down on the pleasantly remembered scene — rocks and pine and scurrying clouds reflected in the swirling green water, trees standing motionless along the canyon rims and clinging to the island in the river.

For the first time he experienced a stirring of pleasure, almost of homecoming; and this surprised him, because he had fallen into the habit of forgetting there had really been a good many happy years for him here, before the final catastrophe of Hal St. Clair's death had abruptly ended it all.

He rode ahead, more memories returning as the cloud-dotted range unfolded before him. But they were bittersweet at best; nothing could change the manner of his leaving this country — nor his greeting on returning to it. He touched the aching marks of Harry Doyle's fists and his eyes were bleak and narrow at the recollection of last night.

He fell into a stock trail, that forsook the river gorge for easier grades down the long slope of the valley. The sun moved over, the shadows of tree and bush shortened to high noon, and the brown range became warm despite the edge of the pummeling wind. Martin dismounted to check one of his mount's rear hoofs and found it had picked up a small stone between frog and shoe; he dug it out and was about to take the saddle again when he heard the sound of another rider approaching at a rhythmic canter. There was something urgent in the drum of hoofs, beating off the sounding board of the rocky trail ahead; with a sense that it was better, on this range, to take no chances, he drew the chestnut aside and placed it between him and the trail. He set a hand on the butt of his holstered six-gun and stood like that, waiting.

The rider came into view, briefly, through a screen of brush where the trail climbed a rise. Martin lost the figure again for a period of minutes, then picked up horse and rider a second time — foreshortened as they topped out of a swale, much closer now.

A sudden constriction of breath swelled Ed Martin's chest. At first he didn't actually believe he could be right, that it was only some prompting of wishful thinking. How could he be so certain, after all the changes a dozen years must surely bring? It was unreasonable.

But his certainty was something older and stronger than reason. It was in the slogging of his heartbeat, in the sudden shaking of the hand that kept his horse snubbed on a tight rein. And then that other horse was full upon him, and the rider was pulling back in startled surprise at the sight of him standing there in the shadow of the pine branches.

"Ed Martin! It isn't really you!"

"Yes, Eve," he said. "It really is!"

Her face was pale, so that her eyes looked like a blue stain against it. She swung quickly to the ground, but having done so she stood irresolutely staring at him, the reins in her hands. When Martin took a step toward her she actually drew away and he checked himself; for a moment, then, neither could do more than stand motionless, facing one another in the warm noon stillness.

"They told me you were back."

He couldn't keep the edge of harshness out of his voice. "Who told you? Was it your pa? Or Arch Casement?"

"Neither one, actually," Eve said. "It was Charlie Runyon. You remember Charlie?"

"Sure. I remember him. I didn't even know he'd still be around. I'm glad to hear it."

"Charlie got it from one of the crew, that they'd run into you in the hills yesterday. I guess Pa must have told them not to mention it to me. But Charlie got the impression you'd been hurt." Her troubled frown searched the marks on his face, the swollen eye. "It was a fight?"

"Hardly what you'd call a fight." He touched his jaw, gingerly. "A fellow named Harry Doyle worked me over — while two others held me for him!"

White teeth caught at her lower lip as she hesitated over the next question. "Charlie said he heard — Doyle was following orders from Pa. That isn't true, is it?"

Martin nodded, and saw the humiliation and pain in her eyes. "Sorry, Eve. It's true enough. The old man sat and watched. They didn't let up on me till I was out on my face, in the mud!"

She gasped and dropped her eyes, as he looked at her. The years, Martin thought, had done her nothing but good. They had taken a coltish youngster and made a woman out of her, with a woman's figure and the assurance of maturity. There could be no question that she was Owen St. Clair's daughter; she had the St. Clair coloring and proud manner, and the fine blonde mane that she wore drawn back and clubbed at the nape of her neck by a bit of black ribbon. But the strong, almost hawkish features of the old man had been somehow softened and muted, in her, to a striking beauty that was wholly feminine. As she stood before Ed Martin now, the wind along the slope molded her blouse and riding skirt against her in a way that made it hard to keep his eyes upon her face, under the flat-crowned sodbuster held by a whangstrap beneath her stubborn chin.

"I was hoping," she said now, "that it couldn't have been quite as bad as Charlie told me. But I had to know. And so, I decided I'd have to see for myself. . . ."

"You mean, you'd have ridden all the way to Gold Camp? Just to see how badly hurt I was?" He shook his head in wonder. "But you didn't have to worry," he added. "The Rileys found me and took me in. They took good care of me."

Martin saw her eyes go cold. "They did, did they?" The change in her was abrupt and startling. Not knowing what he had said or done to make her angry, he watched in astonishment as she turned and prepared to thrust her riding boot into the stirrup, and swing astride her little golden mare.

"Wait!" he exclaimed, and moved to stop her. "At least you'll let me thank you," he insisted, as she again faced him. "For going to all this trouble — for someone you hadn't seen in a dozen years!"

"I'd have done as much for anyone," she said in that same coldly puzzling tone. "If I thought the St. Clairs had hurt him, more than — than —"

"More than he deserved?" Martin completed the sentence, and saw her look away. "Does that mean, you agree with your pa that I'm to blame for what happened to Hal?"

"Oh — I just don't know!" she cried and flung out her hands. "You *did* go there, that night — to Riley's."

"Yes, I went," he agreed soberly. "I don't aim to hide behind a dead boy's back, even though it's true that it was Hal's idea and not mine. I could probably have talked him out of it. It will always be on my conscience that I didn't."

"Well, it's over and done. It doesn't matter any more who was to blame." But from her tone he knew very well that it did, and that there was really nothing more he could say. "It was all so long ago. . . . And you're a lawman, now!" She seemed suddenly anxious to change the subject, to get away from unpleasant memories. "I've wondered, so many times, what became of you after you left the Warbonnet. I remember, I used to watch the mail. I thought perhaps you'd write."

"I did," he told her. "Any number of times. But I always tore the letters up. I guess I figured nobody here would want to hear from me."

"That wasn't true!"

He shrugged. "When Owen kicked me out, he made it pretty plain he thought I'd come to no good end. I meant to show him he was wrong. I guess I had an idea of coming back some day, as somebody pretty big — maybe proving he hadn't been wrong to take me off the range and give me those years of rearing like one of his own. But, I soon found out that was easy to dream about but hard to bring off. I drifted around, pretty near starved for a while. Worked for cattle outfits mostly. Then, by a sort of accident, I landed a job as undersheriff in a railhead town in Kansas. Drifted into law work, that way. And then the federal marshal at Denver saw something in me he thought he could use. . . ."

"And you thought Pa would be proud!" Eve's face showed genuine sympathy. "And instead, he —"

"Oh, no!" Martin said quickly. "Don't think I came back here to throw my weight around. I'm over *that* idea! I decided long ago it would be better if I never set foot on Warbonnet, again. But, there was a job that had to be done — and my boss picked me. If he'd have let me off, I wouldn't be here. Believe me!"

"You're looking for that crazy killer our enemies hired — to slaughter our stock and murder Bill Hammer. . . ."

"I'm afraid your pa's jumping to conclusions about that."

Her fair, winged brows drew down. "Maybe you think it was us that hired him?" she retorted indignantly.

"Now, did I say that?" he answered, gently reproving. "It's just that I never think it's wise to make accusations against anyone, without some kind of proof."

"No — of course not!" She nodded, contritely. Then she added: "But Pa and the crew are terribly worked up! I hear there was even some shooting, at Riley's!"

"There was. A puncher Tom Sheridan had with him took a bullet — I don't know how serious. I'm just hoping there hasn't been anything further, that I don't know about!"

"Nothing that I've heard of. But — Ed!" She lifted her eyes to him, anxiously. "Where's all this going to end?"

"I wish I knew. . . . Tell me this, Eve," he added. "Was it your pa's idea, or this fellow Casement's — putting fence on their land?"

He felt her quick reaction. "I don't see that it matters," she retorted, as though it were a touchy question with her. "It's all land they own or have leasehold on. They haven't broken any laws, have they?"

"That's what I told my boss. Still, it's a coincidence that their wire cuts off all the regular river crossings, so that your neighbors can no longer reach the government graze north of Warbonnet."

"*You* talk about jumping to conclusions!" she said sharply. "Just because Pa was always generous about letting the others cross Chain Link, they forget that it never was more than a privilege! But now, with the range so poor, he has every right to protect what grass he has left."

Martin started to answer something, checked it. "All right, Eve. We won't quarrel about it." There were arguments on both sides, but plainly Owen St. Clair's daughter had been so thoroughly indoctrinated with the old man's particular point of view that it would be fruitless to spoil these moments of reunion by arguing. Instead, he asked, "All these years, Eve — did you ever think about me? Ever, at all? I mean — other than as the man who may have got your brother killed?"

The question startled and threw her off guard. Her head tilted slightly and he saw a faint tide of color tinge the curve of her cheeks. She even stammered slightly. "Ed, it — it isn't fair to ask me that!" And then she broke off, as she saw his glance move past her.

Ed Martin caught his breath, and his whole body stiffened. He reached out a hand, placed it against the girl's arm and moved her quietly to one side. He stood, then, confronting the man who sat saddle not a dozen feet away, silently watching them.

Chapter Seven

He would never know how the fellow had managed to come up without either of them hearing his approach. The rider was Harry Doyle, and at sight of the fists that had beaten him into insensibility the stirrings of red anger began deep within Martin. But he held them back. He looked into the man's jet-black eyes, and at the gun Doyle held slanting down at him, across his saddle swell.

It was the girl who spoke. "Put that gun away!" Eve St. Clair exclaimed. "What are you doing here — *spying* on us?"

The man's blunt brows puckered, as though in indignation; but his tone held mockery. "Spy on you? Why, Evie, you know I never do nothin' without your pa orders me to."

"Are you saying he *sent* you after me?"

"Well, now, somebody seen you taking off from the ranch, in a hell of a hurry. When

Owen heard, it somehow entered his mind that you might be meaning to head for Riley's. That's a tough place, up there. He figured somebody should be along to look out for you."

Martin said, in a hard voice, "What you really mean is, he wanted to be sure I didn't have a chance to talk to her!"

The black stare rested on him. "You was told not ever to go near Evie — remember? You was given a little something last night to make you stop and think before you tried it. It don't seem to have done much good. Looks like you might need another lesson!"

"Not from you!" Martin gritted.

"I only follow orders," the puncher said, in that same mocking tone. "I'm just gonna take you in and let the old man decide how to punish you." He waggled the barrel of the weapon. "First off, I'll ask you to take off that belt and holster. And keep your hand away from the gun."

"Stop this!" Eve cried, in indignation and alarm.

But the muzzle of that other gun held steady. With Doyle watching his every move, Ed Martin deliberately thumbed the prong free of the buckle, flipped the heavy, brass-studded belt and filled leather pouch from around his hips. "Now, buckle it again, and hang the works up here on my saddle horn. . . ."

Still not speaking, face expressionless, Martin looped the belt and fastened it on the buckle. He moved forward then, lifted belt and gun and hooked them over the pommel of the Chain Link puncher's saddle, while Doyle's gunmuzzle peered directly down into his face.

And then, without so much as a flicker of an eyelid to telegraph his move, he grabbed a solid handful of the man's clothing, and jerked sharply as he stepped away again.

Doyle gave a shout, feeling himself going. He made a wild flourish with the sixgun, but Martin was ready for that and he struck the wrist a sharp blow with the edge of his hand. The gun was sent spinning end for end in a smear of sunlight, and then Doyle struck the ground, off balance from his fall. Martin hauled him erect and there was savage satisfaction in him when his fist drove a crushing blow into the middle of the man's face.

Torn loose from Martin's grip, Doyle was hurled back against his saddle. He caught his footing, swore, and threw himself at the other man. There was a startled outcry from Eve St. Clair as the two came together, toe to toe, their fists working.

Doyle had only been stung to fury. He was a tough fighter, even when an opponent's arms weren't being held for him; but Ed Martin brushed aside his blows as though they were nothing at all. His own right fist, boring in, took Doyle in the ribs. The man grunted and, swinging wildly, caught Martin one on the side of his exposed jaw that staggered him. The world spun about him, the sun faded as though some great cloud had slipped across it.

If the Chain Link man had followed through, he might have had his enemy beaten in another moment's relentless attack. But the attack didn't come. Shaking his head to clear it, Martin fought his way past that bad corner — and heard, as through muffled cotton, Eve's sudden cry. Then his vision settled and he saw what Doyle was up to.

The man was fumbling at the gunbelt Martin had hung on his saddlehorn. He dragged the gun awkwardly from the holster and whirled about with it, an ugly look plastered over his bloody features. "Now, damn you — !" he croaked.

It was a reckless chance, but Martin was in no mood to weigh the odds. Even with a gun on him, he waded in; and luck stayed at his side. His opponent's reactions were still dulled and slow, apparently. He stared at the man lunging toward him, as though he didn't believe what he was seeing. Too late he tried to jerk the weapon up — and Martin's bruised knuckles took him in the chest and a second blow smacked against the point of his jaw, with a sound like a hand slapping a side of beef. Doyle's head jerked back; his arms flew wide. The gun in his hand went off, drilling a shot uselessly into the ground. Then the man's eyes rolled back and his lids drooped, fluttering; his knees buckled and he fell straight backward, and his head struck the ground and bounced with a force that made Ed Martin wince.

Martin stood over him, breathing hard, left hand aching enough to make him think he'd broken every bone in it. He shook his fingers slowly as he stared at the man he'd felled; but there was no fight left in Harry Doyle. Eve, standing to one side with a hand raised to her throat, looked white as death. Her eyes seemed fascinated by the smoking six-gun in Doyle's limp fingers.

"Did he mean to use it on you?" she asked shakily.

"I dunno. I wasn't going to wait to find out!"

Moving slowly because his own limbs had a tendency to tremble, Martin picked up the Remington and took his belt and holster from the man's saddlehorn, strapped them about his waist. He pulled off his hat, ran numbed fingers through his hair, and looked uneasily at the girl. "I'm sorry you had to watch that. But I had all I could take off of him. I lost my temper. . . ."

She shook her head a little, with a helpless gesture of her hands. "After what he did — I can understand." She touched her tongue to her lower lip. "How bad is he hurt, I wonder?"

"His skull must be thicker than I thought." The man on the ground was already stirring. He groaned, smeared a hand across his bloody face and up into his hair, and groaned again. He was floundering, trying to sit up, when Martin put a hand under the man's armpit and hauled him to his knees. Bleared eyes wavered to a focus on Martin's face, as the latter scooped the puncher's hat out of the dirt and jammed it on his head.

"On your feet!" Martin grunted.

He got Doyle up, walked him to his horse, and hooked one of his hands limply over the saddlehorn. Grimly, and with a minimum of help from the groggy puncher himself, he hoisted him into leather. There, Doyle managed to hold himself by clamping the pommel in both fists. He still hadn't said a word.

"If you can stick it," Martin told him roughly, "your horse at least knows the way home. Now — get!" He slapped the Chain Link horse sharply on the rump. The animal tossed its head in protest and started off at a shuffle, and the rider's shoulders shook and his head bounced on his chest with every jogging step.

For a moment, Martin and the girl watched horse and rider move away from them, on the downward trail. Then Eve said, "He doesn't deserve it — but I'd better go along and make sure he doesn't fall off the saddle."

"I'd better go with you. This range may not be safe, just now, for you to ride alone."

"No," she said quickly. "I'll be all right. And I can't have you coming to Chain Link with me. You've had enough trouble with Pa. I don't like to think of what might happen if we should run into him!"

Martin started to say something, reconsidered. "All right," he said. He went and got the six-shooter he had knocked from Doyle's fingers; returning with it, he found Eve already mounted and he passed it up to her, standing close for a moment at the shoulder of her little mare. "Take his gun.

As I remember, you know how to use one."

Their hands met as she took it from him, and the touch of her fingers was cold. But she smiled, briefly, looking down at him, and for a moment the distance of time and circumstances fell away as she said, "I should know how! You spent hours teaching me to knock tin cans off fencerails."

A grin broke the line of his own lips. "That's right," he remembered. "I sure did." He looked at her hand, brown and firm and strong. He touched a finger to it, ran it lightly across the back of her knuckles. "We had some pretty good times," he said slowly. "You and me and —" The name caught in his throat. "And Hal. . . ." He dropped his hand, but he didn't turn away. There was something he had to ask her, though the question was bitter on his tongue.

"Yesterday, Arch Casement told me that the two of you were — were promised. . . ." He looked into her face, and saw the guarded look that came into it. "Is that right?"

She hesitated and then nodded — almost defiantly, he thought. "Yes."

"Do you love him?"

He searched her eyes, and saw them turn from his own. "My ma married my pa when she was sixteen," Eve said in an unsteady voice. "You know how old I am? Nearly twenty-seven — an old maid, practically! A girl can't — can't wait around forever. And Arch is the best-looking, best-educated man I know on the Warbonnet . . ."

"But do you *love* him?"

The deliberate and persistant question struck at her, and wouldn't let her off without an answer. Martin saw her eyes cloud, thought he saw her mouth tremble with uncertainty. But then her lips firmed; her head lifted and her hands tightened on the reins.

"You don't think I'd marry one of Chain Link's enemies?" she retorted, too loudly.

Then, before he could think of an answer, the heel of her riding boot struck the mare's flank. The animal broke into a canter. Shod hoofs spurted dust against Martin's legs as he stepped back and watched her ride away from him, her shoulders firm, her eyes straight ahead.

He stood a long moment looking after her; far down the trail, now, Harry Doyle swayed loosely to the jogging of his homeward-moving bronc. . . .

Arch Casement, in the foulest of tempers, left the cookshack at Rafter 9 that noon without having spoken more than a dozen words to any member of his crew. The beauty of the cloud-swept day was lost on him, as he moved at his forthright, solid stride toward the low log-and-fieldstone house. His head hurt still, from the clout he'd taken from someone's gunbarrel when they collided in the dark, up there at Riley's. And it didn't help his mood any to lift his eyes to the pine-topped rise behind the house and see there the mound of dark earth that had been raised over Bill Hammer that morning, on his orders.

There had been no sentiment in the burying, no nonsense about prayer or preacher. If Hammer had a family anywhere, no one knew of it. Casement had let the boys divide up his belongings and had named Bud Flint as the new foreman in his place, with orders to keep the bulk of the crew close, for the next day or so, while they waited to see if there were to be any repercussions over that shooting at Gold Camp.

But Hammer had been more than a mere foreman; his loss was a serious one. Casement was reluctant to admit just how serious.

He walked up the three wide steps and entered the main house, that was still fitted out with the shabby furniture he'd taken over from its previous owner, a hardluck rancher named Tuthill. The condition of this place, that was now his temporary living quarters, made little difference; involved as he was in the process of parlaying a small hand into big winnings, this had been no more than a base for further action — why worry too much about the state of things at Rafter 9, when soon enough he'd be ensconced in St. Clair's big house at Chain Link, as St. Clair's son-in-law? The one part of the house that held real significance for him was the rear room he had had fitted up into his idea of an office, with a massive desk and deep leather chairs and a box safe in one corner; here he liked to spend the small hours of his nights, checking his progress and laying plans.

It was here that he went now — and halted on the threshold to stare at the man who sat in his own chair, at his own desk, waiting for him.

Pale and oddly compelling eyes, in a face as narrow as a wedge, returned his look in silence, raising a cold prickling along the roots of his back hairs. Recovering from the first shock, Casement turned to peer quickly into the hall behind him and then silently closed the door and put his shoulders against it. "Good God!" he exclaimed hoarsely. "How long have you been here?

Did anyone see you?"

"No one sees me," Mort Browder answered cooly, "unless I intend for them to." He added, "I wanted a parley. I thought, if I waited, you'd be coming in here eventually."

"Where's your horse?"

The narrow chin jerked toward one shoulder, in a gesture that could mean anything. Probably it meant Browder had left his mount somewhere in the timber, beyond the working area of the ranch, and then managed to make his way unobserved into this house and this room. Despite himself, Arch Casement felt a touch of the chill and uncanny awe the man never failed to stir in him. But he was determined not to let him know it.

Besides, he was angry, and now the violence that had been backing up in him swelled and threatened to spill over. He walked to the desk and, looking blackly down at the other man, said, "You certainly played hell yesterday! In the name of all that's holy, did you have to turn your gun on Bill Hammer?"

The pale eyes showed no flicker of emotion. "He was crowding me. You know I won't be crowded!"

"I had to make *some* show of giving you a chase! St. Clair got ahold of the sheriff and raised such a storm over those steers you shot, it would have been damned suspicious not to appear to throw in with him."

"How do I know this? Looked to me more like a double cross: I do the job on that jag of Chain Link beef — and next thing, you're helping the law run me through the hills. When that Bill Hammer of yours got too close, I thought I'd best leave you a little reminder of who it is you're dealing with."

Arch Casement ground his jaws. He couldn't say to this man, "I only set you after St. Clair's beef because I knew you had to kill *something!*" He found his hands were clenched and aching, and he opened the fingers and spread them flat along his pantslegs. "There's no double cross," he said tightly. "Remember, you dealt yourself into this game."

"Try to deal me out," the other warned, "and your friend St. Clair might learn a few things he doesn't know. Things like, where you got the kind of money you've been throwing around the Warbonnet!"

"You wouldn't do that to me!"

Casement's big hand shot forward and seized the other's shoulder, in a squeezing grip. Browder didn't even look at the hand, nor did his expression change by a breath. But when he said quietly, "Take it off!" the big man let his arm fall quickly away.

Rage and frustration mingled in him with the underlying, secret fear he couldn't completely hide from himself. It was wholly unfair, he told himself in what amounted to a flash of smothering self-pity, that the past should exact tribute of the present in this manner. Had been a time ten years ago — back in the thin beginnings — when Mort Browder had been very useful to him, in ways Browder never intended. But to be saddled with him now was an embarrassment and a monstrous imposition.

He knew the thought showed on his face, because the pale eyes narrowed and the thin lips quirked slightly. "I've waited a long time for a chance to square with you. Half of that bank loot you walked away with ten years ago belonged to me; so by my figuring, I've got a half interest in this spread and in every other single, solitary damn thing you're promoting for yourself, here on the Warbonnet! Just don't think you're going to sell me out again!"

Casement straightened. He put up a hand and ran the fingers through crisp black hair and let the hand drop to his side. His shoulders lifted and settled again as he drew a breath. "All right," he said heavily. "We went through all this last week, when you first showed up here. We reached an understanding then and it still stands — if you just don't do some damned crazy thing to blow me out of the water!

"I'll lay it straight across the board for you: This place I managed to buy, and the other properties I've got under lease — they aren't worth a damn to me, in themselves. They took every cent I had and I'm going in deeper every month I try to hang on to them. But I'm playing for the big stakes! I've got to keep St. Clair in line, keep our wire on those river crossings and the shirt-tail ranchers shut away from government graze. Because, the more trouble they make, the more the old man turns to me. I have to wait it out while Sheridan and the rest go broke, one by one. And then, when I marry St. Clair's girl, not only Chain Link but a whole range drops into my lap!"

Lean fingers drummed silently on the desktop. The narrow head nodded. "You always had big ideas, even when you were just another out-at-the-seat range tramp rolling drunks in back of saloons. I thought that, when I hitched on with you. I thought it even after you pulled that double cross and left me holding an empty bag.

"Well, it looks like you're sitting up to the big game, this time. You'll either make the killing of a lifetime, or else end up right back where you started. I'm willing to wait and see which way it turns out — and collect my share if there's to be any collecting."

"Then for God's sake don't forget whose side you're betting on! Don't go killing any more of my men!"

"You should have told your men to lay off me!"

Casement spread his hands. "Damn it, I couldn't do that! Only about half this crew is mine by choice. The rest, I inherited when I bought the ranch — for appearance's sake, I couldn't afford to fire every rider on the payroll. If they should get wind of something going on between us, it would soon be all over the valley. It could ruin me!"

"Is that really why you held your tongue?" The eyes probed his. "Or was it something else? Maybe you were thinking you'd have a chance to get rid of me some way — that maybe I'd get careless and turn my back to you, just once. And there'd be no one who knew enough to ask any embarrassing questions. . . ."

Casement felt the revealing tide of color flow into his cheeks. And Mort Browder, seeing his guess confirmed, smiled faintly and eased up to his feet.

He had none of the awkwardness natural to many gaunt men; his loose-hung frame, within the dark range clothing, moved with a studied, almost pantherish grace. He took a canvas windbreaker from the back of the chair and slipped into it, hitching the skirt back with a practiced gesture to clear the polished gunbutt jutting from his hip. Knowing that gun, thinking of the uncounted men who had died in front of it, Arch Casement found his eyes drawn to the weapon with a kind of dreadful fascination.

Then the killer was slapping him gently in the chest with the brim of a flat-topped black hat he'd taken from a corner of the desk. The pale eyes locked his glance in a look of cold warning. "Just remember, Casement — if that's the name you're going by now. You're not going to get rid of me. You won't know when or where, but I'll always be around to watch whatever's going on. Last night, in the hotel at Gold Camp — I'll wager you didn't know I was where I could hear and see everything you said and did!"

Casement could only stare. "Nobody's that much of a damned ghost!"

"I saw you with the marshal that's looking for me — this Ed Martin." The gaunt head wagged slowly, from side to side. "Naturally," he chided, "you wouldn't even *think* of trying to help him find me? *Would you?*"

Casement closed his eyes a moment. His head was beginning to ache slightly, a dull throbbing centered in that place where the gunbarrel had connected. "You're talking nonsense," he insisted, "if you think I'm any friend of Ed Martin's! Him being on the Warbonnet just now can mean real trouble — for me as well as you!"

"Then perhaps we'd better be rid of him."

"If you want to tackle the job," Casement said quickly, "help yourself; it would be time well spent. But don't make the mistake of giving him too much rope — you'll find he's pretty tough."

"We traded some lead last night," the killer said. "I think I got an idea how tough he is."

He seemed to consider a moment. Then he nodded. He pulled on the black hat, walked to the door and paused there, holding it open. "Get on with your business," he said. "I think you can forget about the marshal."

After the panel closed Arch Casement stood for a long moment listening for the sound of Mort Browder's steps retreating down the hall, but hearing only silence. He straightened his shoulders, unable to repress an uneasy shudder — the after effect of that cold, compelling stare.

He supposed it was too much to hope that Browder and Martin could somehow manage to eliminate one another for him. . . .

Chapter Eight

As it could so dramatically, at this altitude and this time of year, the weather changed even while Ed Martin was riding deeper into the Warbonnet. A sheet of slate-gray cloud, with a chilling wind behind it, began to slide in over the rim of the plateau on the north. He saw a wedge of geese burst from beneath the edge of it and draw a wavering line across the sky, throwing down their thin and distant music; they vanished, beyond the southern ridges, and then the cloud-sheet slowly advanced until it presently swallowed up the sun and turned the brown valley floor bleak and drab. Martin fastened the buttons of his canvas coat.

He had been wondering just how this range would impress him, now that he had seen so much more of the world. Time had had its effect, all right. It would seem almost to have leveled off the surrounding hills, to have narrowed down the expanse of the valley from what he had remembered. Still, this was a sizable piece of winter range, even if the current cycle of dry seasons showed in thinning graze and shrunken watercourses, and in the gaunted look of such cattle as he passed.

Easy to see that the Warbonnet ranchers were going to take another beating before spring came again. Due to the drought, few would have had a chance to put up much winter feed; and they would find the cost of hauling it in prohibitive. Worse yet, with streambeds and tanks nearly empty it was an open question what some of them were going to do for water.

As though to give point to his thinking, Ed Martin now ran directly up against the drift fence itself — the one that had heightened the trouble by cutting off access to the river crossings. It gleamed dully in the clouded daylight, its three-strand panels stretching directly across the wagon road where it was broken by a gate. A sign gave terse warning: STAY OUT. As Martin hauled rein a rider eased out of a clump of trees and moved up to the fence, a Winchester carbine cradled in the bend of his left arm. He made no threatening move, merely waited for the stranger to declare himself.

Martin looked at the Rafter 9 on the

shoulder of the roan gelding. He said, "Friend, maybe you don't know it's against the law to fence off a public thoroughfare."

"This is no public road," the man said. He had mean and truculent eyes, under heavy brows that grew in a solid line across his face.

"It used to be. Used to be a town at the end of it."

"Town's still there," the man said shortly. "But the road doesn't go there no more. It ends at Rafter 9. You can go around — ain't out of your way. Much."

Martin had already noticed the newer track sprouting from the old one, to run southward along the fence. He said coldly, "What happens if I'd still rather take the old way?"

"You can try." And the rifle barrel swung slightly and its muzzle settled on Martin's chest. He considered the weapon, making no move toward his holstered Remington.

The guard said, "I got strict orders. No one rides through that gate uninvited. Boss didn't go to all the trouble and expense of stringing wire, for the fun of it."

"And what if somebody doesn't feel inclined to stop?"

"A couple of shots from this rifle will bring me all the help I can use!"

"That's a straight answer," Ed Martin admitted, and he swung his chestnut's bridles into the new trail.

He rode alongside the wire, without haste and without looking back despite the uneasy tightening of the muscles across his shoulders. At last he did turn in the saddle, just for a look; the gate guard had turned his horse and was sitting, still as a statue against the bleak grass, watching him. With the chill north wind in his face, Martin returned his stare across the distance. Then he rode on, and a dip in the ground put the Casement rider beyond his range of vision. . . .

Like the valley, Warbonnet town seemed to have shrunk a little from his memory of it. The streets looked narrower, and somehow there didn't seem to be as many of them.

Much remained unchanged. Some business buildings showed the attrition of the years. On the other hand, the bank had moved into a new brick structure; and Orr and Rath's Mercantile had expanded, with a big frame warehouse overflowing onto an adjoining lot. There was a new hotel since his time. An entire block along one side of Main had a completely unfamiliar appearance: he decided it must have been replaced after being burnt out, in one of the periodic fires that were the common menace of these Western towns with their wooden buildings and their kerosene lamps and woodburning stoves and poorly-fitted flues.

As for familiar faces, in the time it took him to ride half the length of the street and dismount at the hitching rack before the sheriff's office he saw not a single one that might have been somebody he'd known. And, perhaps, he was just as well pleased. He was beginning to wonder if there could be anything but hostility now, between him and the people of this town and this range.

One of the buildings that had changed not at all was the jail, still just as he had remembered it — a squat, ugly building of logs, rather small to be a county lockup. A gray feather of smoke whipped at the stove-pipe chimney, buffeted by the cold wind that tore along the housetops. And when he opened the iron-reinforced slab door and walked into the sheriff's office, the heat of a roaring fire in the corner stove seemed enough to send him back on his heels.

The interior was drab enough — poorly lit by the small, barred windows, and with a heavy odor of disinfectants from the cell block in the rear. At the desk, under one of the high windows, Sheriff Burl Adamson looked up from his writing and scowled in recognition; from the look of him, and from the heat of the stove, he was still thawing out after his ordeal in the rainswept hills yesterday.

Unfastening his coat, Ed Martin said, "Looks like winter may be jumping the gun on us. There could be snow in that cloud sheet, coming down from the north."

The other said crisply, "You have business with me?"

"I was just wondering if you'd heard the details of what happened after you left us yesterday — what we ran into, up at Gold Camp. I figured you deserve to know. If nobody else has already told you, that is."

Adamson could be seen to struggle inwardly, during a silent moment while the fire crackled and roared and pushed its waves of heat into the room. Finally an unbearable curiosity won out, even over the whipped pride of a man who had been ignored and hated to admit it. The sheriff's heavy jowls stirred as he shook his head. "No," he said. "I hadn't heard. What did happen?" His glance settling on his visitor's discolored face and swollen eye, he added, "Looks like it mostly happened to *you!*"

Martin waved that aside. "That was only a little misunderstanding." He slacked into a chair beside the desk, cocked one boot over the other knee and hung his hat on the toe of it. And while the sheriff listened he outlined, briefly, what had taken place at Riley's. He minimized his own set-to with St. Clair and Harry Doyle. He finished by saying, in all sincerity, "I only wish you'd been there with us — the hell with St. Clair! An extra gun on the side of the law could have kept things from reaching the blow-off point.

"Now that blood's been drawn — even not knowing how badly that fellow Rayburn was hit — I rode down to the Warbonnet this morning half expecting to find things had gone to pieces and war had started in earnest. We're just lucky it hasn't. Luckier, maybe, than we deserve to be."

Those other eyes narrowed; the mouth pulled down, between the folds of flesh that bracketed it. "You keep saying 'we,'" Burl Adamson echoed, sharply. "What makes you think you figure in this? You're only supposed to be after that madman, Browder. If you really traded lead with him last night, at Gold Camp, then I don't know why you'd be looking for him down here!"

"I certainly doubt that I scared him away — if that's what you mean!" Ed Martin retorted. "Mort Browder has some stake in affairs here on the Warbonnet. I don't know yet just what it is, but whatever, he's deeply involved — and that means I have to be, too. It's up to you to say whether I'm to work with you, Sheriff — instead of against you."

"What you're really saying, is that I was right all along! The marshal's office has decided to stick its nose into our local affairs!"

"I won't lie to you. We're afraid this is no local affair; not with killers like Mort Browder mixing in it. We hate to step on anyone's toes. But we do want Browder — and aside from that, we're anxious to see the trouble settled before we might have to send an army in."

The sheriff's mouth tightened in anger. He leaned forward and slapped both hands, palms down, onto the top of his desk. "We need no army! Take Browder, if you can find him — but then get your damned federal marshal's badge the hell out of my county! There's no trouble here that Warbonnet law can't handle!"

"You expect me to believe that?" Martin snapped. "Yesterday I heard Owen St. Clair order you home, and you went. That didn't sound too much like the law was in control!"

Burl Adamson's head jerked back, as though he had been struck a blow. His flabby cheeks lost color and then slowly turned beet red. Ed Martin felt almost sorry for him — almost ashamed of himself for having to take such a cruel jab at any man's pride.

Then, before the sheriff could stir himself to make answer, the street door burst open and a clot of men tramped into the office.

They were Tom Sheridan, Luke Frazee, and a couple of others who evidently belonged to their crowd. One of these looked vaguely familiar, but the other was a stranger to Martin. Frazee, wearing a heavy sheepskin coat, kicked the door shut and with a look at the roaring stove told the sheriff, "Man! You got it hot enough in here!" Not waiting to be invited he strode over and closed the damper.

The roar of fire in the pipe was instantly cut off and metal began to give out popping sounds as it started to cool. Frazee turned and went suddenly motionless, then, seeing the previous visitor. And, with all their eyes on him, Ed Martin plucked the hat off his boot toe and got easily to his feet.

So far the sheriff had made no move to greet the newcomers, or ask their business; he appeared to be still trapped in the emotions of the scene they'd interrupted. It was Tom Sheridan who spoke, in a gruff and cautious tone. "Well, Martin?"

The latter nodded briefly, testing the temper of these men who had it in their power to shatter the precarious peace of this range. Their faces were bleakly sober but told him nothing, as Sheridan said, "You know Steve Byam? And Murray Lennart?"

Lennart was the one he'd remembered — the name came back to him, just as he heard it spoken. He had been a thin-edge kind of operator who ran a hundred head or so of beef over toward the southwest end of the basin; to judge from his appearance, the years hadn't done much to improve his condition. Neither he nor Byam offered to shake hands now. They returned Martin's look in a silence that was vaguely hostile; yonder by the stove, Luke Frazee's glare of enmity could hardly be mistaken.

Martin spoke into the growing silence. "Sheriff and I were discussing that affair at Riley's, last night."

This seemed to break through to Adamson; the desk chair creaked under the man's soft weight as he stirred himself. "That's right," he muttered. "Martin, here, says you got a man hurt — young Rayburn, I understand. How about it? Was it serious?"

"He's not going to die, if that's what you mean," the rancher answered curtly. "He took a fairly clean hole, in the leg — lost some blood and had a painful ride home. I got him in bed now and my wife's looking after him.

"But all this is beside the point, Sheriff! What matters is that we were minding our own business last night, not bothering anybody — and then Casement and St. Clair and their riders came storming in and threw down on us, and began their bullying. Seems to me the law owes a man protection against such treatment."

Adamson peered at him through lowered brows. "Is that the reason you're here? If you intend preferring charges against Rafter 9, for your man getting shot, seems to me it would be hard to prove. Martin, here, tells me there was a lamp busted, and it was dark when the gunplay started. . . ."

" 'Martin, here, tells you!' " Luke Frazee broke in, his tone heavily sarcastic. "Looks like he's really pumped you full! Who the hell's running this office? Him, or you?"

That touched Adamson on an already sore nerve. He lifted a trembling finger at the rancher and fairly shouted, "Now, look here, I don't have to listen to that sort of talk!"

Frazee started a heated reply but Tom Sheridan stepped in then, shouldering him aside. "Forget Ed Martin!" the grayhaired man said sharply. "Happens he's not the only witness. Joe Riley was there."

"Riley won't help you much," Martin said, ignoring the blinded rancher's baiting. "He has no idea who shot Rayburn; neither does his wife — I asked them. Try to make anything out of the evidence you've got, and Casement can argue that it was one of you accidentally shot your own man."

"We're asking the sheriff, mister!" Frazee retorted. "Not you!" His one good eye shone with pure malevolence; his mouth twisted. "That hunk of tin on your chest must sell pretty damned cheap! How much did you get from Casement, to go along with him to Riley's and back his trumped-up charge?"

"I don't think you remember so good." Ed Martin had to keep his own voice under control. "I never backed Casement. I was there hunting Mort Browder, not any of you. Maybe you've forgotten Casement and I had a row — and when reasoning wouldn't stop him, I did it by knocking a lamp off the bar."

"An accident!" Frazee retorted, from a depth of dogged prejudice. And then Tom Sheridan spoke again, while Martin was still trying to find words that would have some effect on this man with his battered face and his stubborn, twisted hatreds.

"You still sticking to that Browder story, Martin?" Sheridan's tone was quieter than his companion's but just as much freighted with distrust. "I hate to call anybody a liar, but it's the only name I got for the man who says we could have brought that killer in here. I don't care if you do wear a badge!"

Ed Martin returned his stare, and it was like looking squarely at a brick wall. He swung his glance and saw the same expression reflected in all of them. He looked at Burl Adamson sitting like a lump, impotent and scowling, in the chair behind the desk. He dragged on his hat, as a sudden wave of futility crashed over him.

"Nothing I say seems to make any impression," Martin told these men, "so I might as well save my breath. You wanted to see the sheriff — well, I'll leave you with him."

With his hand on the doorknob he hesitated, nearly turning back; but then he shrugged, said "Oh, hell!" and walked out of there before he let himself say something worse. Yet as the door slammed behind him, he knew a dark suspicion that he'd done more than merely miss an opportunity.

This was just the sort of scene he'd instinctively dreaded, from the moment he was first handed this assignment. Plainly, the past was still very much a part of him; in losing his temper with those men, he had lost a battle with himself. . . .

Chapter Nine

Ed Martin returned to his horse, at the rack in front of the sheriff's office, and stood there in the gray and windy afternoon trying to down his anger and think ahead. He felt like a man in a box, with no clear direction and with his mind blurred by frustration and fatigue.

He had ridden down here today, tensed and not knowing what he could expect to find after the blowup at Gold Camp; and simply because he had not found a shooting war — at least not yet — his body was reacting and he felt the letdown. His punishing of Harry Doyle had helped cancel out last night's beating, but it hadn't erased the physical aches. He was tempted to retrace his steps to that new hotel he'd seen up the street, check into a room there, and sleep the clock around.

He couldn't do that, of course, but at least he could spare himself a quarter of an hour. Across from the jail, sandwiched between a couple of store buildings, was a small square structure with a paint-peeling barber's pole next the door. He remembered there had been a tin bathtub in the back room of that shop, and suddenly the thought of soaking the soreness from trailweary and battered muscles was infinitely inviting. He led the chestnut across the street.

The barber was new since his time but the tin tub was still there. Very shortly Ed Martin's long length was stretched out as best it could, luxuriating in steaming warmth and in water as hot as the man would heat it. He scrubbed down well with the strong yellow soap, and thought he could almost feel the soreness slipping out of him.

Afterward, as he stood naked on slippery duckboards rubbing himself down with the coarse towel, he heard voices out in the shop and heard his own name spoken. Instantly cautious, he eased over to where his clothes lay folded on a stool with the holster belt on top of them, and slid the Remington free. He was holding it ready as the curtains parted and Tom Sheridan peered at him through drifting layers of steam. Martin lowered the gun. Still badtempered from the scene in the sheriff's office, he said, "This is a public bath but it's not that public!"

Sheridan bobbed his head in apology. "Sure — sure. Just wanted to make certain it was you — I thought I saw you come in the shop. We'll be waiting out here when you get finished. We want to parley."

"More talk? What's the good of that?" Martin said harshly, but he shrugged. The head was withdrawn and he finished toweling and started to dress. When he went barefooted out into the shop, he was carrying his gunbelt and boots and buttoning his shirt.

They were waiting. Murray Lennart was seated in the barber's chair, legs crossed and one boot swinging. The rancher named Byam lounged on the bench against the wall reading an old magazine he'd found there. Tom Sheridan turned now from his spread-eagled stance at the window, where he'd been looking out upon the windy street.

The barber wasn't in evidence. The "CLOSED" sign hung in the window; apparently these men had sent him off somewhere so they wouldn't be interrupted.

Ed Martin was curious but he wouldn't show it. He slung his gunbelt over a wall hook while he proceeded to work at the buttons of the shirt. He said, "Well, how'd your talk with the sheriff go?"

Sheridan shook his head, and shoved the

rope-scarred fingers of a hand up through his crisp, gray-sprinkled mop of hair. "It didn't. Adamson made it pretty damned clear we can't expect a thing from him."

"I'd have told you that. He's out of favor with Casement and St. Clair, just now; but I think he figures he can get back in if he's careful not to do anything more to cross them. This was the wrong time to ask him any favors."

"We want no favors!" Lennart said indignantly. "Nothing more than our rights!"

Martin only gave him a look and stuffed his shirt tail into his pants, cinched up the belt. Sheridan, watching him, gnawed at the inside of his lower lip. He said suddenly, "Look! We know we're out of line, acting the way we been. We're sorry. If you tell us Mort Browder killed Casement's foreman, then we've got to figure you know what you're talking about — even though we still insist we had no part in such a killing. Anyway, we're here to apologize for seeming to doubt your word."

"Yeah?" The marshal looked around. "Looks to me somebody's missing. . . ."

"You mean Luke Frazee." Sheridan nodded, admitting it. "I got to ask you to excuse him, Martin. He was a different man, six months ago. It's no joke to have an enemy lay a quirt across your face and leave it ruined, like that — the sight dead in one eye. . . ."

"I heard he was caught trying to cut St. Clair's barb wire. The old man always was too handy with that quirt. But, I wonder if you deny he had a right to put a fence on Chain Link?"

He saw the rancher's mouth tighten. "Will you listen to our side of it?"

"Why not?" Seating himself, Ed Martin proceeded to pull on his socks and boots. Sheridan watched him a moment, scowling, before he began to speak.

"These are lean times, on the Warbonnet — three dry years in a row. Unless we get a lot of snow up in the hills, one more winter will likely see every little outfit like ours fold up and die. By comparison, St. Clair's in damned good shape. You know his setup. He always did have the best graze, by virtue of getting here first; his patents control three out of the five good crossings where stock can get down into the canyon and make it over to the other side. . . ."

The rancher went on, "But the rest of us are desperate, Martin! Our cricks are all but dried up; we face the winter with no graze for our herds and no cut feed to carry them. Happens, there's still grass in the sheltered draws of that plateau country north of the Warbonnet; we figure it could at least carry skeleton herds through for us — and moreover it's on government land, free graze supposedly open to any man's beef that needs it. Trouble is, last spring this fellow Casement turned up from nowhere with a pocket full of cash. He bought out George Tuthill's old place on the river, changed the brand to a Rafter 9. He took leases on a couple of other ranches lying between him and St. Clair's Chain Link — and the next thing that anyone knew, the two of them had put up a drift fence that extended clear across their front and cut us clean away from the river crossings."

Stomping his heel into a boot, Martin said, "I've seen the fence."

"Then you've seen what it does to us. But Casement and St. Clair claim it's legal, and they dare us to try anything. When Luke Frazee tried, he was beaten and lost an eye."

Martin said, "But the fence *is* legal. It's all on their own land."

Leaning forward tensely in the barber's chair, Murray Lennart retorted, "Its purpose is to keep us away from free grass! Then, after we've all gone broke — they divide Warbonnet between them!"

"Have you tried the courts? Asked them

to declare eminent domain and force a way for you to reach those crossings?"

"The courts!" Lennart spat onto the worn linoleum. "We could all starve to death before they'd move!"

The man named Byam said, "We know now the sheriff isn't going to do anything. It leaves only you."

"Me?"

"That's the size of it," Tom Sheridan agreed, nodding soberly. "We don't want a war — but we're being pushed into one if we hope to survive. You, though, have the power of the federal government in back of you. What about it, Martin? Will you help us?"

"Against Owen St. Clair?" Ed Martin leaned back on the bench, laid a quizzical stare on the rancher. "I wonder. . . . This remind you of anything, Tom?"

"Can't say I know what you mean."

"Eleven years ago, there was a kid who got into trouble with St. Clair. The old man horsewhipped him and kicked him off Chain Link and ordered that nobody on Warbonnet should do anything to help him. And, they didn't! They blackballed the kid — every last man in the basin. As a final hope he went to you, Tom. He thought, if anybody would, you'd have the courage to stand up to St. Clair and tell him he was doing wrong. But, no — you turned the kid away!"

This recital had had an extraordinary effect on Tom Sheridan. He appeared to grow taller as his body stiffened and his head went back. A flush of color spread across his cheeks and his mouth settled firmly between the lines that bracketed it. For a long moment he stared at Martin while the room seemed to hold its breath; the only sound was the ticking of a tin alarm clock, on the shelf that contained the barber's array of tonics and shaving mugs.

Tom Sheridan's chest swelled as he filled his lungs. He said through tight lips, "Maybe you think I haven't lain awake a lot of nights, with the shame of that gnawing at me? Well, you've finally had your revenge, I guess. You've thrown it in my face!" He added stiffly, "I won't bother you again." And while the other pair of ranchers stared, unmoving, he turned and yanked the door open. Gusting wind nearly took it out of his hand.

Then Ed Martin said gruffly, "Come back in and close the door!"

Slowly the rancher faced him. "Even a kid has to grow up," Martin said in a cold voice. "Was a time I thought I hated this town —

and this range, and everybody on it. I still got no love for any of you; but just now that's not important. *This* is." And he touched the badge pinned to his shirt.

As Sheridan pushed the door to, Martin got to his feet, took his belt and gun from the wall hook and slung them in place about his waist, settled the holster. "You say you want no trouble with Casement and St. Clair. Honestly, does that jibe with slaughtering Chain Link beef?"

"None of us has done any slaughtering!" Sheridan answered flatly. "Any more than we killed Ed Hammer. We've tried our best to keep the peace. But, push a man too hard and he may have to strike back."

"Well, that's an honest answer," Martin admitted. He put a boot on the edge of the bench, leaned to rest a forearm on his knee. He considered each of these men in turn. He said, "You know — if you're really sincere about this — it's occurred to me while we've been talking there may be a way to prove it. A way to get what you say you want, without the need of any fighting."

"We're waiting to hear it!"

"All right. You maybe know a place on the Warbonnet — I remember we used to call it 'Rocky Point.' There's an island in the river, that makes a good deep pool. . . ."

Murray Lennart said quickly, "Over toward the east end of the valley? Where the river comes out of the hills?"

"You've got it." Martin nodded. "I remember I used to fish that hole, as a kid; I'd get to it by way of an old deer track, down the south bank. This morning, coming in, I stopped for a look and I could see there's been a slide, and the trail's wiped out. But I have an idea that with pick and shovel, and maybe some powder, that trail could be opened again — and even widened so as to make a drive trail for stock. What's more, the water's quiet enough there that I figure it's a place it wouldn't be too hard to push them across."

Sheridan eyed him narrowly. "Build our own crossing? Bypass Casement and St. Clair and their damned drift fence? Is that what you're suggesting?"

He nodded. He could see the notion intrigued them — any idea was bound to, if it offered the least sign of hope; any plan was better than the frustration of doing nothing. Tom Sheridan looked dubious, though Steve Byam said, "It might work. I know a guy with the railroad who might be able to lend me some mules and a couple of fresnos. But time's awful short. . . ."

"You surely don't think for a minute,"

Sheridan demanded, scowling, "that Casement and St. Clair would sit on their hands and let us get away with this, once they had wind of what we were up to?"

"They'd have to go outside the law to stop you," Ed Martin pointed out. "And that's where I'd come in." He turned, took his hat and windbreaker from the wall. He looked again at the three. "Well, anyway, I told you my idea. Whether you're going to do anything about it is your decision.

"Meanwhile I've got my own job: I've got Mort Browder to find — and I won't do it, standing here talking!"

Since he had a clue, at least, in that shoe with its twisted frog, the obvious thing was to look for sign of it. By making a swing across the head of the valley, Martin believed it should be possible to cut Browder's trail and thus determine if and when he actually rode down into the Warbonnet. But the job was bigger than it might look. These hills were honeycombed with stock trails and with draws debouching out of the timber, any one of them a route the killer could have used. Too much of the day was already gone, and the heavy cloudsheet brought down a cold and murky twilight to end his search before he had more than half begun.

Ed Martin still had some supplies left. He made camp in a glen of rock and trees, close enough to one of the main trails that he would know of any travel over it during the night. As he was breaking branches for his fire, in growing dusk, he thought he felt the cold touch of moisture against his face; but if there was snow in the wind it apparently amounted to no more than a few vagrant flurries, that quickly passed. And by the time he had his fire, with coffee at the boil and bacon sputtering, the wind had dropped away and the flames made a pleasant room of warmth in the dark immensity of trees and night and mountains.

So still had it become that he could hear every sound his horse made on its picket rope — the popping of the chestnut's ankles as it moved slowly about, the grind of jaws tearing the tough grass. But the sound of the gun came utterly without warning; he would always wonder how the ambusher could have got so close to him without detection.

He never did know why that first bullet missed — perhaps the flicker of the firelight, washing against the face of the boulder behind him, made him a deceptive target.

For what could have been a fatal count of seconds he sat with tin cup half raised, the steam and the aroma rising into his face. Then he broke loose of the grip of surprise. He flung the cup away, while a boot lashed out and kicked the fire apart. He dived for the shadows as though he were diving into water, and lit rolling. A second shot drilled the night and this time he heard it strike the rock somewhere above him; by then he was on his belly, facing toward the muzzleflash, and his gun was in his hand.

He fired twice, putting his shots waist high and about a yard apart. After that he was rolling again, and brought up only when his hip struck a length of down timber. He pressed close against this and waited, not breathing, as he tested the dying echoes of the gunfire for further sound.

There was nothing. Even the horse, over there on its picket, had been startled to inaction. Martin was as certain as he had been last night, up at Riley's, that his man was Browder. But last night Mort Browder had been trying only to escape; now, he was stalking his enemy's camp, and Martin didn't doubt for a moment that he was set and determined to make a kill.

The chill of the ground, still damp from recent rains, began to work its way into his prone body. He lowered his gun. There was a faint glow from the fire he had scattered, where a couple of sticks continued to burn and send sparks wavering toward the black sky. He found his eyes had adjusted to it, so that this mere hint of light seemed bright enough to blind him to anything beyond it. He shook his head and squinted his eyes to clear them — and realized he had been watching, without actually seeing it, a dim figure that stood motionless just within the circle of fireglow.

There had been no sound of an approach. He was so surprised that it was a moment before he remembered his gun and grabbed it up; but even as he did so, the figure moved on out of sight, drifting toward his own left.

He didn't risk another shot, not wanting to offer a target; at the same moment he realized the peril of letting himself be flanked. At once he began to scramble backward, crawling swiftly on knees and elbows, and cursing the noise he made. Getting to his feet he stepped into the protection of a pine tree, put one hand on its cold, rough bark while his other fisted the gun. He kept his breathing light and shallow as he listened.

There was the sudden muffled crack of a

trodden branch. Martin snapped up the gun and fired blindly, then ducked as an answering bullet thudded into the pine trunk. Afterward, tired of this game, he left his post and started running straight toward that other gun. There was another shot, that missed him widely. He triggered at it and then dropped to one knee; remembering he had only one bullet left in the Remington, he hastily jacked out the spent shells and reloaded, working solely by touch.

He completed this process, and still there had been no other sound from his enemy. No good in waiting for Browder to grab the initiative; better to keep pressing and throwing him off stride. Martin slowly came up to a crouch and then straightened and took a tentative step forward. Just as he did so he heard a shot, and a second one. They weren't aimed at him. They came from farther off than he had expected, over toward the flat beyond his camp. Puzzled, he held up, juggling the gun in his hand and listening to the silence that had come down complete again.

Then, suddenly, understanding came crashing in on him. "No, by God! Even he wouldn't do that!" But he mouthed a curse and hurried recklessly forward.

Dark as it was out there on the grass, he

almost stumbled over the body of his horse. He dug out a sulphur match and, made careless by anger, popped it on a thumbnail. One glance showed him the glint of light on a sightless eyeball, the dark shine of blood. Stiffening legs made a last spasmodic movement; the chestnut lifted its head and then lowered it gently and all motion ceased.

At the same moment, some shift of wind brought a murmur of hoofbeats striking off rock somewhere in the night, the sound quickly passing. With bleak fury in him, Martin dropped the match and put his boot on it, grinding it hard into the earth. He shoved the Remington back into holster.

"Couldn't get at me," he said through clenched teeth, "so he shot the horse! What kind of a monster does he call himself?"

Emotion spent itself at last and, in the letdown of aborted physical action, he walked back to what was left of his fire. He started to kick the half-consumed embers together, then checked himself with a shake of the head. Instead he gathered his pack, and afterward went and picked up his saddle and blankets.

Most likely Browder was through for this night, but there could be no sense in counting on it. Rather than give the killer another opportunity, he was going to have to find himself a new camp, without a fire. It meant a cold night, and then the dismal prospect of a hike awaiting him in the morning.

Chapter Ten

Dawn came as a slow and sullen leakage of gray light through the overcast, that was far denser than it had been when the sun went down; the clouds lay heavy upon the forest and the mountains, swollen with what Martin judged must be a tremendous freight of snow. The wind had fallen off to nothing, so that the air seemed softer and almost warm until the slow chill, taking its time, gradually inched its teeth into him. There was that sensation of breathless waiting that heralds the coming of a storm in winter.

But if the season's first snow was on the way, it held off. Martin, who had slept fitfully, broke camp with the first hint of daylight. He shook the hoarfrost from his blankets, ate a cold breakfast and then made up a pack and cached it where he should be able to find it again. At the thought of the hike that lay ahead he was tempted to leave the heavy stock saddle, as well; but he decided he had better take that along — there was always a chance he might find a horse running loose and manage to put a rope on him. So he hefted the saddle, settled his shoulder under it, and started walking.

He had been trying to decide what was the nearest actual place where he might expect to pick up a mount — it wouldn't take many miles of this kind of travel, on boots not exactly designed for hiking, to convince a man he wanted to cut it as short as he reasonably could; and to that, just now, was added the danger of finding himself afoot in the middle of a blizzard. Had Tom Sheridan and the others taken seriously the idea of digging a crossing at Rocky Point, and actually set their crews to work at it, then of course that would have been his likeliest hope. But at best it was uncertain.

Probably he'd find nobody at the Point, would merely end up tacking on extra miles that he could spare himself by heading directly toward the nearest ranch headquarters, which should be Arch Casement's Rafter 9. He realized there was no telling what kind of a reception he was apt to get at Casement's. On the other hand, this was an excuse to have a look at what the man had been making of the ranch he'd bought.

So when he left the timber he set a course, as direct as memory allowed, toward the headquarters of what had been George Tuthill's spread.

He kept plodding doggedly, switching off to the other shoulder whenever the saddle became too heavy or muscles too cramped. The breath hung in a veil of mist before his face. The windless, nearly soundless day lay about him with the feel of winter; the lumpish, heavy sky marched with him, and so did the slow hours. But the snow held off.

He came at last to the familiar line of three-strand barbed wire fence. There was no gate at this point and, for all he could see, no guard. Martin simply dropped his saddle across the fence and crawled through. Now on Rafter 9 land, he felt a need for renewed wariness — even if he was the law, and even if he had a sound reason for being here, he could expect to be reckoned as a trespasser. And this time when he lifted the saddle, that felt as though it had doubled its weight since he started, he was careful to hoist it onto his left shoulder so as to leave his gun hand free.

He had never been really familiar with this section of range. He did remember that George Tuthill, the original owner, had not built his headquarters directly on the river even though he owned access to it; the Warbonnet was too unpredictable, too apt to flood when spring runoff of melt water from the hills sent it rampaging, chocolate brown and dangerous, down its swift channel. Tuthill had played it safe and chosen a picturesque spot for himself above the steep bluff — in a timbered pocket, open toward the south, where low rounded hills helped protect his buildings from the worst of the winter winds.

Coming to it now, along one of the many irregular horseback trails that converged on the ranch headquarters like the spokes of a wheel, Ed Martin approached from a direction that brought him almost in on the place before he realized it. The first hint that he was even close was when he came around the flank of a brushy slope and saw the buildings lying in a clump below him — main house and barn and bunkshack, and the corrals and outbuildings that made up the heart of a working ranch. He halted abruptly, lowering the saddle to rest his shoulder a moment as he stood there under the gray sky, studying the layout.

The windows gleamed faintly, giving back the dull half-light of the day; motionless fingers of smoke rose from various chimneys. A half dozen horses stirred in the corrals. He saw a man leave the barn and cross the bare yard to enter the bunkshack, and now the thin, metallic clang of a smith's hammer came to his ears. But those at the ranch just now were apparently staying pretty much inside — it was that kind of day.

Martin stooped to take up the saddle again, and suddenly went motionless. He sank to his knees in the thick brush, to watch a pair of men he had at that moment discovered.

It was a wonder he'd noticed them at all — only some motion or fleck of color had caught his attention. They stood just within a fringe of timber, on the near side of a low knob of ground between him and the ranch buildings, and from this angle they appeared foreshortened and partially hidden by pine branches; but one of them was, plainly, Arch Casement. Martin recognized him easily since the rancher was bareheaded, in vest and shirt sleeves. It looked almost as though he'd got a signal — from the top of that wooded knoll, perhaps — that brought him out here in such haste as not to bother with either hat or coat.

The second man, back farther in the shadows, wore a windbreaker and a wide-brimmed hat that shielded his face. Martin thought briefly of the glasses, cached with his other belongings in the hills, and swore a little wishing he had them now. But next moment he didn't need them — the man lifted his head and he got a clear look at the narrow face beneath the hatbrim.

It was the face he'd seen in a police picture, in Hendryx's Denver office. No doubt of it — Casement's visitor was Mort Browder!

There appeared to be an argument afoot. He saw Casement raise a clenched fist, saw the other knock it aside with a gesture that made the saddled horse behind him toss its head. Martin hadn't noticed the horse until that moment; he got a look at it now. It was a sorrel, all right.

He touched the gun in his holster, but nothing less than a rifle would be any use against Browder, at this range. And it would have been too late then, anyway.

Casement stepped back, as the other turned to his horse and swung into the saddle. A final word and Browder whirled the sorrel and gave it a kick that sent it off into the trees. Casement stood a moment looking after him; then Martin saw him heel around and start back across the knoll in the direction of the ranch house. As he went he swung his arms vigorously — either in anger, or because he had just now realized he was cold.

The sorrel and its rider came into Martin's range of vision again briefly, leaving the timber and crossing an open swale. A lift of ground carried them from sight; the faint drum of hoofbeats faded. Martin came slowly to his feet, a hundred unanswered questions crowding into his head.

Well, one thing remained unchanged: He still needed a horse, and this was still the only place where he could hope to get it. Once he had a saddle under him, would be time enough to think about the problem of somehow bringing Browder to earth.

More keenly aware than ever, now, of the risk he was taking, he loosened his gun in the holster, stooped and hefted the saddle and got it onto his shoulder again. He was starting forward when there was a sudden shout, behind him. He turned, halting, and saw a rider silhouetted on the comb of the ridge spur — a black figure against the dull, slaty clouds.

"Hold it, you!"

The man's voice came down the stillness, a harsh challenge, and then the rider set the hooks to his horse and sent it buckjumping down the slope, smashing through brush and raising gritty clouds under the jar of its pistoning hoofs. Ed Martin stood and let him come, not lowering the saddle or trying to draw his gun. The rider pulled the reins with a quick sawing motion that jerked the cow pony around, hard, and pulled it to a broadside halt.

Dust spurted and through the thin, saffron fog of it he looked up into the scowling face of the man he knew as Bud Flint.

"The marshall again!" Flint's voice was heavy. His stare raked the figure of the man standing before him, touched the saddle propped upon his shoulder. "Lost your bronc. An accident?"

"You could call it that," Martin said. "I been hoofing it since dawn. This was the closest place I could think of, where I might borrow another."

The man's expression showed no change, no easing. "That'd be up to Arch," he grunted. "Keep walking. We'll see what he has to say about it."

It was both an invitation and an order. Martin took it as such, and without further talking turned and started on down the slope. He could hear plainly the slow thud of hoofs and creak of saddle leather, as the rider eased his mount into a walk behind him.

Descending, they lost the ranch buildings for a while behind that wooded rise where Casement and Browder had held parley;

then the trail brought them around into sight again. They circled a corral and moved down one long side of the barn. As Martin reached the forward end, he at once saw Arch Casement again, talking to a couple of his men.

Casement, still in shirtsleeves, had his hands thrust deep into his pockets while his elbows clamped his sides and his shoulders hunched slightly against the cold. He glanced up at the newcomers, started to look away; then his eyes snapped back again and fastened on Ed Martin's face, in a hard stare. Slowly, he straightened.

The marshal halted and let the heavy saddle slide off his shoulder to the ground. "Look what I found, Arch," said Bud Flint gruffly.

"Can't you read?" Casement demanded, his eyes boring into the lawman. "Or don't you believe in 'No Trespassing' signs?"

"I didn't notice any sign," Martin said coldly, "and I wouldn't have let it stop me if I had. It's too far, to walk to town."

Other men were drifting up — rather a lot of them, he thought, to be hanging around headquarters on a work day. To Martin's eyes they fell sharply into two types; and he pondered this. Some were plainly working cowhands, a little more down-at-heel than some. But there were others — more than half of those he saw — who seemed to hold themselves apart, as though they considered themselves a superior breed. These were men of Bud Flint's stripe — men who wore their gunharness with a flair and gave the impression of being at least as handy with it as with a rope. Among them he noticed the towhead, Whitey Lewis, with a patch of bandage showing under the brim of his hat.

He had seen working ranches, and he had seen outfits that were frankly collections of paid gunhands. This Rafter 9 of Casement's appeared to have the features of both. . . .

Casement was studying the marshal, his truculent stare narrowed in thoughtful concentration. He spoke to Flint, who had not yet dismounted. "Where'd you find him?"

"Picked him off the ridge trail." Flint indicated the rise of brushy slope with a backward jerk of his head. "Before I seen the saddle, I figured he was spying."

Mention of the ridge had a quick effect on Casement. Martin saw the rancher stiffen, and bring his hands out of his pockets. He cut a glance toward the ridge, and his thought could not have been plainer if he had shouted it. Martin told himself, he's wondering if maybe I *was* spying — if I could see him and Browder, there in the trees. . . .

It seemed a good idea to get the man's thoughts away from that area, and quickly. "All I want," he said, as Casement's look came back to him, "is the loan of a horse. Like I said — it's a long walk to town."

The rancher was in no hurry to answer. For a long and cheerless count of ten, his gaze continued to probe the lawman as though trying to strip away the words he spoke and read the mind behind them. "What happened to you?"

He knew he had better be careful to tell the strict truth, on the risk that his hearer might have heard it already. "Somebody jumped my camp, last night — tried to put a bullet in me. When he couldn't do that, he put it in my horse instead and set me adrift. I don't know for sure, but I have an idea it was Mort Browder."

Bud Flint made a scoffing sound. "Browder! Chief, he's still fiddling on *that* string!"

Casement simply ignored this. His face was devoid of expression. He said, with a shrug, "I'm not the one to throw obstacles in the way of the law — so long as it keeps its nose out of my private affairs! Sure, you can have the loan of a bronc, Martin. Flint, go fetch him that little dun out of the barn corral, and let him put his saddle on him. You and Whitey Lewis have chores in town to take care of, so you might as well ride along with the marshal and one of you can bring him back with you."

Martin was watching Flint, and he saw the slightest hesitation as the man heard his orders — the look of a man who was puzzled. But the expression was gone so quickly that it might almost have been imagined; Flint nodded curtly. He told Whitey Lewis, "Saddle up. I'll fetch the dun." He pulled rein, twisting his mount around and sending it toward the pen where several head of stock were running.

A comment from Casement brought Martin's attention back to the Rafter 9 owner. "You don't seem to have been having a lot of luck. Any thought yet of giving up?"

"Give up on Mort Browder?" Martin shook his head. "Less chance than ever. What was only a job gets to be something a little more personal, after you've been shot at and set afoot!"

The other was looking at the discolored marks of bruises, and the left eye that was still swollen. "Browder do that to your face, too?"

"That was something else again." He didn't bother to elaborate, and a moment later Bud Flint came riding up from the barn leading a dun gelding, a likely enough looking animal. The Rafter 9 men watched in silence as Martin piled on his gear and swung astride. He settled into the stirrups, nodded at Casement. "Nice horse. I'll try not to get this one shot."

"You try hard," Casement said, with a short laugh.

Bud Flint and Whitey Lewis were waiting. The Rafter 9 crew — that odd mixture of out-at-pockets cowpunchers and hardcases — watched impassively as Martin nodded and touched a heel to the dun. It responded with a good show of spirit, and quickly settled beside Bud Flint's horse as the latter led the way out of the ranchyard, into the wagonrutted trail that plainly was the main road to Warbonnet town.

Chapter Eleven

Within a quarter hour of quitting Rafter 9, Whitey Lewis's bay horse began to show a remarkable tendency to hang back. The first time this happened, Martin simply drew rein and brought them all to a halt, putting the blame on his own mount: "Me and this fellow don't seem to get our signals straight!" The three went along well enough for a while after that, with Martin riding the comb between the wagon tracks and the other two flanking him on either side of the road.

Then Whitey began to drop behind again, and this time anger tightened Martin's lips; he suddenly pulled up, swinging the dun so that he had both his companions in sight. He laid right hand significantly on the butt of his holstered gun and told the blond rider, "Let's just cut out the nonsense! I get uneasy when somebody's riding in back of me!"

Despite himself, Whitey couldn't prevent the guilty flush from pouring up into his cheeks. He shot a look at Bud Flint; but the latter was sitting with both palms piled carefully on his saddlehorn, an obvious indication he wasn't choosing this moment to challenge the marshal. They sat there under the sullen sky, forming a triangle, with a chilly hint of breeze sighing along the brown earth and tugging their hatbrims and plucking at the manes of their horses.

It was Flint who said, with an attempt at a sneer, "Marshal sounds jumpy."

Martin, not deigning to answer, held his challenging stare on Whitey Lewis and, after a moment, the towhead shrugged and gave the bay an angry kick. Martin reined the dun around as Whitey fell in beside him; they went on, then. But now a clear and uneasy tension lay upon the three, with the Rafter 9 men silently groping to reopen damaged channels of communication.

After a moment, Ed Martin said quietly, "Don't you boys know Casement is making suckers out of you, with his lies about Mort Browder?"

Flint's head jerked around. "Who says they're lies?"

"Supposing I told you Browder was at the ranch? And that I saw the two of them together, only a minute or so before you picked me up?"

After the slightest pause, the other merely shrugged. "And supposing you did? Look! You're not dealing with those two-bit cow nurses he got from George Tuthill. If the boss has got something he's keeping quiet, it don't concern us."

"Doesn't it?" Martin turned to Whitey Lewis and brought a scowl to the blond rider's face by pointing out, "Because you didn't know about Browder, you nearly got your skull smashed for good outside that barn at Riley's. Your friend Bill Hammer came off even worse. But does any of that bother Casement? The minute he knew it was Browder murdered his foreman, he started to stall and hang back — he *wanted* that killer to get away! Is that how your boss looks after his crew?"

The argument seemed to be getting to Whitey. Martin saw him gnaw at his lower lip, and raise a hand to rub the back of his neck and thoughtfully touch the bandage where Browder's gun had struck him down. "It's my notion," Martin went on, pressing it, "that Browder might have something on him. Something from his past, maybe. If that was true, and I was Casement — playing for the stakes he is — I imagine I'd pay any price to keep it a secret. Even to losing a few riders, more or less; what would that matter to him?"

"Shut the hell up!" Bud Flint growled fiercely; perhaps he could see the effect Martin was having on the towhead. Suddenly there was a movement of his arm and a six-shooter was leveled at the marshal's beltbuckle. "You've talked enough," he said, as all three horses lagged to a stop. "Get his gun, Whitey."

"I see," the lawman murmured quietly. "It's like this, is it?" He looked at the gun, his own hands motionless on the reins. Over in a black stand of pine a crow suddenly burst from a treehead and went flapping away under the heavy cloud ceiling, his hoarse cry startlingly loud in this stillness.

"I wondered all along if you two actually had any chore in town," Martin said dryly. "Or if Casement was just signaling, without coming out and giving you your orders in front of those punchers. It wasn't the horse you were supposed to bring back, *was* it, Flint? It was me!"

Flint's mouth was set hard and unyielding, under the heavy mustache. He cut his stare at Whitey, who was still hanging back for some reason. "I told you to take his gun! Now, do it!"

"Sure. . . ."

There was the popping of cold saddle leather and a slur of steel shoes on dry grass, as Whitey edged closer to pluck the Remington from the prisoner's belt holster. Turned reckless and angry, Martin refused to wait. At what he judged the proper moment, his left leg moved convulsively. His spurred bootheel drove hard against the dun's near flank and, with a squeal of startled pain, the animal leaped sideward, colliding with Whitey's bay.

The blond rider was reaching for the gunhandle; his fingers barely touched it. Then the jolting collision of the two mounts flung him off balance, against Martin. The latter made a grab with his right hand for the material of Whitey's brush jacket. The thick stuff slid through his fingers, but he got enough of a grip to complete the work of pulling the man out of his saddle. Whitey yelled, a hoarse shout; his hat tumbled off and pale yellow hair whipped into Martin's face. Then the coat was torn from Martin's grasp as its wearer tumbled to the ground, between their horses.

Martin, knowing the risk of hitting the wrong man was probably all that had kept Bud Flint from shooting, was already grabbing for his own gun. He got his fingers around the grip, pulled the Remington up from the leather — and then there was the explosion of a shot, almost in front of him. His left arm, holding the reins, received a blow that instantly numbed it to the shoulder, and nearly drove him backwards from the saddle. Gasping, he grabbed for the pommel, aware that in doing it he had let the gun slip from his fingers. Just then it scarcely mattered. The dull blanket of numbed feeling seemed to spread from his left side through his whole body. Vision blackened. The dun was moving under him in near panic and he never knew how he kept that right-handed grip on the saddle-horn or held his place on its back.

He had nearly forgotten Bud Flint; then he realized he was waiting for a second bullet and that it somehow failed to come. Instead he became aware of a nearing thud of hoofbeats; and saw that Flint was staring off toward yonder belt of pine timber. Whitey Lewis had scrambled to his feet and had drawn a gun of his own; but in that instant, neither man seemed to be giving much attention to the marshal. With an effort of will he turned his head and saw a rider approaching, at a hard clip, from the direction of the trees. He figured it must mean more danger — it could hardly be a friend.

He looked down to the ground — and there was the Remington, lying in the dry stubble where he had let it fall. He could feel a growing, steady throb of pain as the hurt arm began to thaw; he gritted his teeth and summoned strength to climb down and recover the weapon while his enemies' attention was elsewhere.

Moving in a haze, he dragged his leg up and over and hung to the saddlehorn as he groped for solid earth. The strange horse, already frightened, sidestepped uneasily from the sagging weight and Martin lost his grip on the horn and went down onto his face, hard. He very nearly blanked out. But determination got him to his knees; with the hurt arm dangling uselessly, he looked again for the Remington and saw it a yard away — just out of reach.

Only seconds had passed, actually. Now he heard Bud Flint's angry voice cursing as the man suddenly saw what he was trying to do. He lifted his head and looked into Flint's face, and into the muzzle of the gun swinging toward him. There was the flat report of a rifle. Flint's whole body jerked and then he was flying from the saddle, his arms and legs flung loosely — like a rag doll knocked from a shelf. He hit the ground, and his horse trumpeted and moved away and Martin saw the rider from the trees spurring up with a saddle gun clamped under his arm and smoking from the shot.

The man pulled rein and instantly the long barrel swung toward Whitey Lewis, who stood as though stricken. "Get rid of that!" the rider said. Whitey seemed almost to have forgotten he had a gun in his hand. At the command he looked down at it, a little stupidly. Suddenly he dropped it hastily into the holster as though he had discovered it was red hot.

The newcomer said sharply, "What's going on here? Almost looked to me like I interrupted a murder!"

"It's none of your business," the tow-headed puncher said in a surly tone. "And Arch Casement isn't going to be happy about you interfering!"

"Then let Casement complain. He knows my address!" He shifted his weight onto one stirrup while he leaned for a look at the one he had shot; Bud Flint, lying on his back in the stubble, was stirring slightly and groaning with every quick intake of breath. "He'll live," the rifleman said shortly. "I drilled him high, apurpose." He jerked his head at Whitey as he straightened. "Still, you damn well better get him on his saddle and get him home."

Rifle laid across his thighs, he waited in silence while Whitey went to look after his hurt companion. Flint was in no shape to help himself. With some trouble, Whitey got him hoisted and laid face down across his saddle, hooking his belt over the pommel. Then the blond gunman mounted his bay and collected the reins of the other Rafter 9 horse. Holding them, he looked over at Martin and at the man with the rifle. His mouth opened, closed again as though he thought better of what he had been about to say. He shrugged instead, in an angry and baffled manner, and set off toward Rafter 9 headquarters with the hurt man's bronc trailing.

The one with the rifle watched the horses dwindle across the brown grass; before they were quite out of sight he shoved his weapon into the saddle boot, swung down, and came over to where Ed Martin was climbing to his feet, clutching his wounded arm. He was considerably below the latter's height and he had to tilt his head back as he said, "Well, youngster! They told me you was back."

"Hello, Charlie," Martin said.

Charlie Runyon was an oldtimer — almost as old as Owen St. Clair, for whom he had ridden most of his mature life, but boot-tough. Martin could see no change in him — his face wrinkled and hard and brown as a nut, his eyes clear and blue for all his years, his mouth humorous under its wispy straggle of tobacco-stained whiskers. Charlie, at least, was one who'd never seemed to accept St. Clair's interpretation of Hal's death. He had been a friend of both boys, and his had been almost the only voice raised in Ed Martin's defense.

"Let's see what he done to you," he said now, and Martin obediently worked at the fastenings of the canvas windbreaker so that the old man could pull it back and expose the wound. "That Flint!" Charlie muttered,

"I never did cotton to him. But, hell! I ain't partial to none of that Rafter 9 crew — or the man they work for, if it comes to that! I happened to be over in them trees, when I sighted the three of you; and something about it looked mighty damn funny to me. Glad I decided to wait and make sure!"

Martin suddenly remembered the crow, that had gone flapping out of the pines; it should have been a giveaway that someone was in the trees, but all three of them had missed the significance of it. He started to say something, broke off with a grunt and bit his lip as Charlie Runyon began drawing his jacket off the injured arm. His shirt sleeve was rapidly soaking up blood; Charlie whistled softly, proceeded to rip away the cloth. He peered at the wound closely. "Needs attention, all right. For now, this will have to do." He brought out a handkerchief from his hip pocket and proceeded to make a crude bandage.

"It will have to do, period," Martin corrected him. "I'm riding."

"Sure. You're riding with me — to Chain Link, where we can fix that arm the way it should be done."

Thinking of Mort Browder — thinking of the time that had already been wasted — Martin shook his head impatiently. "It's nothing. Nothing at all!"

"That's what Johnston told 'em, at Shiloh. Albert Sidney Johnston — best general the South ever had, to my way of thinking. He should of won, that day. He should by rights of won the war for us. But he sat under a tree in that damned peach orchard and bled his boot full, just because he was too stubborn to admit he'd been bad wounded.

"I ever tell you, I seen him sitting there? Well, I did. Just a glimpse — no more, me moving up into the line through the shot and thunder, and the peach blossoms dropping like pink snow all over that damned bloody ground. During the night I heard he was gone — bled to death, they told me. I think the whole South began to bleed to death, that day at Shiloh Church!" It was a story Martin had heard the old man tell a hundred times. As he rambled on, Charlie was pulling the knot tight and drawing the bullet-torn jacket in place over Martin's shoulder. "Now, climb in that saddle. You're coming along with me!"

"No!"

But when he put his foot in the stirrup, an alarming wave of giddiness hit him and he knew the other was right: he had lost too much blood already. So he let Charlie Runyon help him to mount, and shoved his left hand into the front of the jacket to immobilize it and ease the pain of the torn muscles. "My gun," he said, and Charlie picked the Remington up and passed it to him. Martin holstered it, and after that Charlie was back in his own saddle. He turned his horse to the south; and Ed Martin followed, not arguing any more now.

Chapter Twelve

Though it was barely noon, the day was growing darker. What little wind there was had dropped away to nothing and when they came in on Chain Link, the motionless fingers of gray smoke rising from chimneys of house and cookshack and bunkhouse were like pillars trying vainly to shore up the swollen, heavy sky.

Ed Martin said, "I hope you aren't forgetting — I've been told not to show my face here."

Charlie Runyon shrugged the reminder aside. "Ain't apt to be anyone around, anyway," he said. "Old man has himself and the whole crew out this morning, making a final check on the fence before a blizzard starts — which it damn well looks like it could do, any minute. He sent me to ride the north end where it runs into Casement's section. That's what I was doing on Rafter 9 when I happened to see you and that pair, and got curious."

"I've noticed there's no fence separating Rafter 9 from Chain Link."

"Oh, hell no." The puncher's voice was sour. "It ain't Casement we're scared of, or those hardcases like Bud Flint he brought in with him. Owen's just afraid of men who have been his neighbors for a dozen years or more! Anyway, why bother to keep their two ranges separated?" he added bleakly. "When it looks like they're all gonna be one, shortly. All in the family!"

Martin shot him a look, that showed the undisguised distaste hardening the old fellow's mouth. It told him plainly enough what Charlie thought of the projected marriage of Casement and Eve St. Clair. He didn't press the subject. . . .

It seemed very odd to be riding again into this place that had been his home for so many years. When he left, he remembered, a big new barn was just in process of building; now the structure was weathered and the first hint of a sag had settled in the high roofline. A windbreak of cottonwoods along the west side of the yard was taller and thicker — otherwise things looked just about as they had. The ranch house had been painted a new color, and there was a picket fence around it that he didn't remember. He saw, up under the eaves, the window of the room he and Hal had shared, when they were boys; the sight filled him with a bittersweet flood of memories.

As Charlie Runyon had said, the home ranch was deserted. A cook, with a white dishtowel tied over his jeans for an apron, came to the door of the eatshack to throw out a pan of dishwater and stood for a moment watching them, then turned and went inside again.

Martin saw his companion starting to rein over to a hitch rack near the bunkhouse and he said, "If it's all the same to you, I'd like to put this bronc in the barn. And leave the saddle on."

That got him a probing look. "You of the opinion Casement might have followed us?"

"I'm of the opinion there's no sense putting up a signpost."

"Might be you're right," Charlie agreed, and led the way into the barn.

Dismounting took more of an effort than Martin would have thought; afterward he put his good shoulder against a roof prop and let it support him while Charlie Runyon led both horses into stalls and slipped the bits from their mouths. "Unsaddling can wait," the puncher said as he rejoined Martin. "First things first. Come along. . . ."

They walked out of the barn — and found Eve St. Clair sitting her saddle, staring at them. Her face was pale as she demanded, "Ed! What are you doing here? Don't you know that Pa — ?"

"Now, just a minute!" Charlie Runyon said sharply. "How your pa acts is *his* business; but I'd think you'd be ashamed, Evie — if only for old time's sake — turning Ed Martin away when he's been hurt. He didn't want to come — I brought him. I'll take him to the bunkhouse and fix him up, and then I'll get him out of here. It doesn't need to bother you, at all."

Whether it was the scolding, or her own belated awareness of the shape Martin was in, an immediate change appeared in the girl. "No — wait!" she cried, and leaped down. She put out a hand toward his arm, beneath the bulky coat, but withdrew it without touching him. She said to Charlie, a little reproachfully, "Did you think I'd turn him away — or any man, that was hurt? He's not to go to the bunkshack, either. Bring him to the house."

"Whatever you say," the old puncher answered mildly, and he turned Martin in that direction. The marshal suspected he was secretly pleased at the rise he'd been able to get from her.

While Eve led her mare into the barn, Runyon opened a gate in the picket fence and led the way up a flagstoned path to the rear door of the house, which happened to be the closest. He held the door open and Martin walked into the kitchen, and at once was overwhelmed by its welcome warmth. The aroma of the big coffeepot, simmering on the back of the wood range, seemed to contain in it the memory of every meal he'd ever eaten at that scrubbed, oilcloth-covered table, of every winter evening he'd spent watching Eve at her work; doing the week's baking perhaps — a chore she had taken on early, after her mother's death. This house, he knew, was forever home — as no other house would ever be.

Charlie Runyon, having closed the door and shut away the chill, motioned him to a chair. "You sit," he ordered, and went rummaging through a cupboard as Martin lowered himself and placed his hat on the table beside him. Charlie returned with a bottle and a glass; he poured the glass full. "Better drink this. You can use the steadying." Martin took it without arguing, welcoming the heat that the whiskey sent through him.

Afterward he had to submit as the old puncher clumsily stripped off his canvas coat. The makeshift bandage was soaked with blood, but when Charlie tried to pull it free it stuck fast. "Gonna have to soak that off," the puncher said, as he saw Martin wince. "Looks like you're in luck, though — it shows the thing's quit bleeding. I better be getting some water on to heat. . . ."

Eve came hurrying in, then, laying aside her own hat and coat. She gave one look to the hurt man's arm and at once took over. They watched as she made arrangements — getting a tin basin from its hook, filling it at the pump. As she opened the stove to stir up the fire, she asked, "Who did it?"

"Bud Flint," the old man told her, and nodded as he saw her look. "You heard me right — Flint, that's just been made foreman at Rafter 9. He was trying for murder. And he'd have finished the job in cold blood, except I was handy and managed to stop him."

Her eyes went big with shock. "You didn't kill him!"

"I don't reckon; I aimed high. He was breathing, last I saw."

"But — still, I don't understand *why!*" She turned her stare on Martin. And for just an instant he hesitated over his answer.

Then he said briefly, "A personal difference," and knew, from the way her expression closed down, she could see he meant to say no more. She let it go, though she frowned as she turned away.

A moment later Eve said, "Some things I have to get. I'll be right back." And she disappeared through the hall door.

At once, Charlie Runyon was leaning to demand, in a fierce whisper. "By God! Ain't you gonna *tell* her?"

"Tell her what?"

"The truth! How Flint and that other fellow was working under orders. And about what you seen at Rafter 9. . . ."

"I can't tell her a thing like that."

"But, dammit, she's got to know!"

"Do you think for a minute she'd believe me?" Martin retorted. "Against Arch Casement? Of course he'd deny it. And he's the man she's engaged to!"

Charlie made an angry gesture, with one rope-burnt claw of a hand. "Engaged!" He mouthed the word as though it tasted bad. "I reckon that's what she calls it; but you can't make me think she's really serious, not if she's ever stopped to think. It's her pa, mostly, who's been putting the pressure on her — Casement's got him thinking he's the biggest thing ever come down the pike. But believe me, if either one of them was to know he's into something with a crazy killer like this Mort Browder —"

Martin's warning hand, clamping down on his wrist, halted Charlie in midsentence. He turned quickly, breaking off as he saw Eve standing in the doorway with cloth and scissors and antiseptic in her hands. How long she had been there — how much she might have heard — Martin didn't know; but he was troubled by the expression on her face, an odd look he was unable to interpret.

Charlie Runyon, for his part, looked as though he either had swallowed his tongue or wished he could. An awkward silence stretched out as the girl came into the kitchen, put down the things she had brought, tested the water heating on the stove to see if it was ready. When she carried the pan over and placed it on the table, Martin could see the tightness in her cheeks, and the slight trembling of her fine, strong hands.

But her fingers were steady enough and her touch infinitely gentle. She worked swiftly and silently while Charlie stood awkwardly about, hindering more than he helped. The bullet wound ran long across the upper arm, half way between shoulder and elbow, but it was a shallow one after all and had cut no major blood vessel. The water in the basin turned red as she carefully bathed it, and then raw alcohol made Martin's whole body jump, hitting the torn tissues. The girl sucked in a quick breath, frowning and biting her lower lip; and though Martin managed a grin to reassure her, he got no smile in return.

Eve finished with a careful binding of clean white cloth, ripped up from a dish-towel. She offered to get him one of her father's shirts, to replace his own that had had a bloodsoaked sleeve ripped out of it, but this he wouldn't consider. The bandage, he said, was too bulky anyway for a sleeve to fit over it. He let her fashion a sling that would hold the injured arm motionless across his chest, and declared it a fine job. And having thanked her with warm sincerity he added, "I'll be going now," and got to his feet.

"No!" she exclaimed. "You shouldn't try, not so soon after — after —" Astonished, he saw her mouth begin to work and suddenly she turned her back to him.

"Why, what's the matter?"

"Nothing!" she answered, too emphatically; her voice sounded oddly muffled. "I'm just being womanish. And all at the sight of a little blood!"

Charlie Runyon gave a snort. "You, Evie? I don't believe it! You've patched up plenty worse than this. What about that time in the corral, when the bull turned on Red Yates and hooked him?"

She didn't seem to hear. "You could have been killed!" she insisted, still not looking at Martin. "Only a few inches more. . . ."

"But it didn't happen," he said, and placed a hand on her shoulder. "So it isn't worth anybody's getting upset about."

He felt her stiffen under his touch. Then she was jerking away from it, lifting her head to show him a face that had lost its color. Her manner was changed, turned curt and practical as she agreed: "No. Of course not."

Ed Martin could only frown, completely at a loss. One moment this girl seemed to be driven by some strong memory of old affection for him; in the next, he could see nothing but animosity. And somehow he sensed that this had little to do with her father, or Hal, or Casement. It was something deeper — between the two of them; something into which no third party entered at all. It was a wall of emotion she erected, and it baffled and bothered him.

He said heavily, "I still think I better be

going." He found he'd lost most of the shakiness that had threatened him. He took his coat off the chairback and shrugged into it awkwardly, letting the sleeve dangle empty above his injured arm. He was reaching for his hat when he heard Charlie Runyon's sudden exclamation: "Hold it! Riders coming!"

They were coming in a hurry. Eve showed him a look of quick alarm as the drum of hoofs swelled; then she was turning and hurrying through to the front of the house, and after the briefest hesitation the two men followed her.

The living room — low ceilinged, filled with heavy furnishings that seemed to reflect Owen St. Clair's forthright personality — lay at the forward end of a hall that split the house from front to rear. A log blazed in the fieldstone fireplace. A big glass window looked out upon the ranch yards; and there, beyond the stretch of lawn with the picket fence surrounding it, a quartet of riders were just dragging to a halt. But they were not Chain Link men. Instead, Martin saw the solid figure of Arch Casement, and recognized three of his crew.

Charlie Runyon let out a gust of breath. "By God, you were right! They're after you!"

"Nonsense!" Eve retorted, before Martin

could answer. But as they saw Casement switch the reins to his left hand, big body shifting preparatory to stepping down at the gate, she suddenly appeared to reach a decision. She flung open the big door, hurried across the deep veranda and down the flagstones. Seeing her, Casement changed his mind for the moment and settled back into the leather; and Martin felt the tension loosen its grip on him a little, took his hand away from the holstered Remington.

"Good for her!" he heard Charlie Runyon mutter. "And good for you, come to think of it," the old puncher added, "suggesting we put those broncs in the barn. Look at him there, giving the whole place the eye! Wondering if you're here or not — but not quite ready to come right out and ask her —"

"Be quiet!" Martin broke in, motioning him to silence. "I don't think that's what he came for. . . ."

Eve stood with one hand on the gate. Across the fence, the mounts were restive, kept moving about under the controlling hands on the reins. A few erratic snowflakes were starting to drift down from the swollen clouds. In the day's unnatural stillness, the voices carried.

"Pa?" Eve said. "Why, no, Arch. He *isn't*

here. He's with the crew. He said it looked like a blizzard coming, and —"

Casement interrupted her. Even from this distance, Martin could see the restless impatience eating at the big man. "You got no idea where I could find him?"

"Well, he did say he expected to noon at the line camp at Three Pines. You know where that is?"

He nodded, lifting the reins. "Maybe I can catch him there. Thanks, Evie."

"Wait!" She pushed the gate open a little, in her anxiety. "What is it, Arch? What's wrong?"

"Nothing to worry you. If he comes in you could tell him there's a little trouble that needs tending to. On the river — place named Rocky Point." And he whirled his horse and was pounding out of the yard with his men behind him, already stretching out into a gallop. Eve stood looking after them.

To Ed Martin, it was as though an alarm bell had suddenly put up a clamor. He was already in motion; his face was bleak as he strode back through the house, into the kitchen where the good smell of coffee brewing on the back of the stove grabbed at him, with a warning that the cold breakfast he'd had at dawn was no longer working for him. But, no time now to think of food. He went on without missing stride, getting his hat in passing. In the barn, he led the dun from its stall and was having trouble bitting up, one-handedly, when Charlie came hurrying in.

"Where the hell you off to, in such a lather?"

"The Point," he said. "It looks like a fight." As Charlie, seeing his difficulty, stepped in to slip the metal into place for him, Martin explained briefly the plan he had suggested for building a new crossing. "Sounds from what Casement said, that Sheridan and his people must have decided to take my advice. And I promised them I'd back them up if it led to trouble."

"You sure you're in any shape to ride?" Martin, not bothering to answer, took the reins and swung into the saddle. "I'd best come with you."

Martin looked down at him. "There's something better you can do, if you will. See if you can find the sheriff and get him out there."

"Adamson?" The old puncher made a face. "I don't see him stirring his stumps outside that office, not in the face of this kind of weather."

"He should be given a chance," Martin

insisted, "to show where he stands. If this is the showdown, he's got to declare himself — one side or the other."

Charlie Runyon appeared wholly dubious, but he nodded shortly. "If you say so." And Martin, feeling the pressure of events, ducked the low doorway and rode out of the barn, into thickening streaks of snow.

CHAPTER THIRTEEN

He was cresting a long roll of open land, a mile or so north of ranch headquarters, when he happened to look back and saw a rider pounding hard after him. It was Eve; Martin gave a groan of exasperation and pulled rein, knowing he couldn't run from her.

The girl came on fast and he saw a riding crop flash a time or two in her hand. Then she was reining in, pulling the mare to a stifflegged halt. They sat and looked at one another for a moment. Eve said, in a small and reproachful voice, "Charlie told me."

"He told you what?"

"Everything! He could never keep any secrets from me. He's always been soft as putty in my hands, since I was a little girl — you know that." She looked into Martin's face, searchingly. "You don't really think there's going to be fighting? Just because the other ranchers might have tried to find a new way to get their stock to the river?"

"Yes, Eve," he said soberly. "I really do."

"But you're so *wrong!*" she cried. "Can't I make you see that? Are you so blinded by your hatred of my pa, that you think he and Arch are *monsters* of some sort?"

He shook his head. "I don't hate anyone," he told her quietly. "Unless it might be the kind of man who'd try to ruin his neighbors, by grabbing off water and grass that by rights belongs to everyone. Maybe Owen St. Clair wouldn't do that. For your sake, I hope he wouldn't. But I can't help it if the signs point different."

The way her handsome blonde head snapped up, her eyes flashing anger, Eve had never looked so much like her father — or, he thought, so magnificent. And then her arm rose, and the riding crop was clutched so tightly the fingers showed white across their knuckles. Martin thought surely she was going to strike him across the face and in spite of all he could do he flinched, cheek muscles fluttering and tightening with the memory of another St. Clair whip he had felt, those many years ago. She saw his expression; she read it correctly. And suddenly, as realization of what she was doing seemed to flood through her, her face turned crimson and she dropped her arm, abruptly.

"Why don't you use it?" he demanded.

She wouldn't answer. "If you're in such a hurry to get where you're going," she said between tight lips, "then you'd better be doing it. Only, I'm going with you."

"I can't allow that. You don't know what we might run into."

She said stoutly, "I keep telling you there's not going to be any fighting. I want to see your face when you have to admit how wrong you've been."

Martin lifted his shoulders and let them fall again; to argue was a waste of valuable time. His jerk at the reins was almost savage. The dun tossed its head and he used his spurs and shook it out into a mile-eating gait. But the girl was close behind him.

Impatient as he was he had to ride warily, for the most direct route lay across Rafter 9 and that must be counted enemy territory. He swung wide of the ranch headquarters; some time later, they reached Casement's north boundary and passed the line of the fence without raising the gate guard — seemingly, he had been pulled off. At least they saw nothing of him, and let themselves through unhindered. Then they were pushing ahead again, with the country roughening toward the head of the long valley.

In all this time, neither Martin nor the girl had spoken. Though they rode so close, they might just as well have been a thousand miles apart. There was nothing to say, no way to communicate across the barrier they had raised between them.

Snow was falling now, still not heavily, meeting the skin of face and hands with a touch that could just barely be felt. It melted instantly against the heated flanks of their horses, but it was starting to collect as a white scurf in hollows and on rocks and brush and trees. The heads of the mountains, butting against the gray roof of the sky, were lost in mist.

Thus they came in at last toward the Point, where the river flowed through a gorge that could have been chopped out of the ground with two great strokes of a giant ax. As soon as they rode out of the timber they saw signs of activity on the canyon's broken rim. There were a couple of wagons, a cavvy of horses inside a rope corral, a couple of sentries moving about a fire. One of these stepped forward brandishing a rifle, and tried to wave them off. But Ed Martin rode deliberately toward him and pulled rein, saying, "Where'll I find Tom Sheridan?"

The lookout hesitated, then grudgingly indicated the canyon with a jerk of his head. "But you can't go down there," he added sharply as Martin and the girl stepped from their saddles.

"Who says so?"

"Damn it, we're just getting ready to set off some powder. . . ."

So they had to wait. After all their urgent haste, it was a galling irritation to Martin. He felt drained of energy; his arm, in its sling under the canvas coat, ached from the jolting it had taken.

He saw a coffee pot heating and remembered he was hungry. Without waiting for invitation he took it from the coals, filled a cup and offered it to the girl who said, with distant coolness, "No, thank you." Martin drank it himself; the hot liquid felt good in his empty belly. But the futile passing of the minutes became increasingly intolerable.

"Has there been any trouble?" he asked the guard. "Any one done anything to stop you?"

"Nope. We did see a couple of riders scouting us, about an hour ago; they kept their distance."

Martin saw the girl nodding triumphantly,

as though this somehow confirmed all her own arguments. It angered him; he shrugged, and tossed aside the empty cup. "Those were Casement's men," he said, gruffly. "Just give them time!"

The lookout told him, darkly, "We may not have much time. This is a big job; the weather could close us down before we —"

A faint warning yell sounded in the depths of the canyon. Moments later the roar of the explosion smote them. The ground shook; a gray cloud of smoke and dust billowed out of the river cut. Then fragments of rock were raining about them and setting the frightened horses in the corral to stirring. Even before the dust had settled, or the echoes of the blast had rolled and bounced away across the hills, Ed Martin was already starting down into the gorge. And Eve St. Clair was close behind him, shaking off his hand when he turned and saw her stumbling over loose rubble.

The men were quitting the cover they had taken, while the powder went off, and were falling to work again. They swarmed like ants across the canyon wall — there must have been a good two dozen of them — and Martin saw they had begun making some progress toward clearing the steep trail, widening it enough that a beef animal could safely use it. The snow was falling faster now. It swirled in the currents of air that eddied here; it spun out of the sky and lost itself in the black spires of pine trees at the bottom of the gorge, and in the dark, sliding water of the river.

Ed Martin found Sheridan and three others gathered in a drift of acrid powder-smoke, examining the results of their shot. A stubborn shoulder of native rock had been knocked out and shovelwork would now clear away the debris. Sheridan, issuing instructions, broke off in mid-sentence when he saw Martin and the girl; not waiting for his stammered question the marshal proceeded to tell these men of Casement's visit to Chain Link.

They heard him out in silence. But as he finished someone came shouldering forward to demand, "And what's the girl doing here?" It was Luke Frazee, his one good eye gleaming with fanatic belligerence. "What business you got bringing a St. Clair with you? Was it so she could spy on what we're up to?"

Tom Sheridan started to say, "That'll be enough, Luke!" But Eve cut him short, answering her father's enemy herself in a flash of anger that — Martin had to admit — made her astonishingly attractive.

"He didn't bring me; he couldn't have kept me away! Before I leave I'm going to hear all of you apologize for the things you're thinking!"

They looked at her in silence, Sheridan with the regretful air of one who had known this girl since childhood — who liked and admired her as a person, and regretted the circumstances that made it impossible for them now to be friends. In the end, since there was no answer that could satisfy her, he simply turned away.

Martin asked the rancher, "How much of a force do you think they can throw against us?"

Sheridan ran a palm across gray-stubbled cheeks. "Hard to say. Personally I have an idea a good half of Casement's men would refuse to fight. They were George Tuthill's crew — they've got little use for the hard-cases they're working cheek by jowl with nowadays. They've only stuck this long because jobs are hard to come by."

"What about Chain Link?"

"Well, that's a different matter. I reckon they'd follow St. Clair through hell. They may not like it much; but if he says fight — they'll fight!"

"Then Casement needs Chain Link," Martin summed it up. "With St. Clair, he has the odds. Without him, he's in trouble."

"I'd say that was about right," Sheridan replied, and there was a sound of exasperation from Eve St. Clair. She moved her shoulders, looked at the sky and shook her head; her arms were firmly crossed and, beneath the hem of her skirt, one boot toe had begun to tap the ground angrily.

Murray Lennart, who was one of the group, said anxiously, "We just going to stand talking and wait for them to catch us, down in this hole? If we've got to fight, we should pick our ground."

Martin had been considering this. There really was no good place to make a stand, unless perhaps they withdrew into the timber above the rim. "Better call your men together," he suggested, and Sheridan nodded and turned, an arm lifting, mouth open on a shout that he never made. For it was in that instant that a ragged outburst of yelling, and then a storm of drumming hoofs and a few crackling gunshots, broke out atop the canyon rim above them.

Obviously, in the suddenness of the attack the lookouts had been caught without time even to give a warning. The men in the canyon, their picks and shovels still in their hands, turned and stared upward through falling snow as the rim suddenly swarmed with figures that had not been there moments before.

Now the solid shape of Arch Casement strode forward. He held a rifle by the balance, and used the other hand to cup his mouth. "You, down there — can you hear me? Then throw away your shovels and your guns and climb up out of that. We'll give you two minutes!"

Looks of dismay passed among the trapped men. It was Tom Sheridan, as their leader, who lifted a shout of angry defiance: "So it's out in the open, at last! You've decided to show your hand — and just like we expected, there's a gun in it!"

"You're in no position to argue!" Casement retorted. "We can wipe you right off that wall into the river, if that's how you want it. Or, are you going to use your heads?"

Ed Martin had to draw a long breath to steady his voice. "Casement!" he shouted. "Is St. Clair there with you?"

"Martin?"

The surprise was evident in Casement's exclamation. He could see the man's head turn quickly, hunting for him. And now the tall, spare shape of Owen St. Clair moved into view, and St. Clair was saying, "What is it you want with me? Speak up — I'm waiting!"

Martin doubted very much that they could make out individual faces clearly, through the swirl of snow in the gorge; he was quite certain neither of them realized as yet Eve was there. Now, as he looked at the girl, he thought he had never seen more eloquent shock and disappointment on any face. It filled him with a savage anger.

But he spaced his words, trying to push common sense past the stubborn blocking of reason inside the old man's head. "You must know you're on Government land, this time. Try to interfere with these men and, for once, you'll have no technicality to stand on. Makes no difference what you think of me, Owen — you can't be foolish enough to fight the badge I'm wearing."

Given a fair chance, the argument might have had effect. But perhaps Arch Casement sensed that, and was determined to push things beyond any chance of turning back. "The hell with this!" he shouted suddenly. "Your two minutes are up!"

The rifle in his hands spat fire, hurling a bullet in the direction of Ed Martin's voice. And that was all it needed.

CHAPTER FOURTEEN

Martin was already in motion, though he knew any shot from the rim would be too high to begin with — firing downhill, a man was almost certain to overshoot his target until he made adjustment. As other guns began to open up he whirled, caught Eve about the waist and bore her down with him into the nearest cover.

Ancient slides, like the one that closed the deer track, had spilled down-timber all across the slope; it was the protection of one of these fallen trees, weathered to a dully gleaming silver, that Martin sought for himself and the girl. Part of the tree's massive root system remained, packed with rocks and caked mud to form an effective shield. Martin knelt behind this. Knowing he would need both hands free, he took his hurt left arm out of the sling, slid it into its sleeve and buttoned the canvas jacket — he found movement was painful but bearable. After that he drew his gun and looked to see what was happening around him.

The first burst of fire from the canyon rim had scattered the working party, into whatever cover they could find. Martin saw one who had been hit and lay writhing with a shattered leg; as he watched, somebody got to the man and pulled him to safety. Behind fallen logs or boulders, a few of them were trying to set up a sporadic answering fire. But the attackers on the rim were taking no chances. They had the advantage, in both numbers and position; they could probably see a quick surrender as soon as the enemy recognized the odds, and so they were keeping low to offer poor targets.

Behind his shield of roots and mud and matted gravel, Martin juggled the Remington and looked over at Eve. She made a forlorn picture, huddled there behind the log with her knees drawn up and hands pressed to her face. Martin knew she was crying — could almost feel the shock and the shame and the humiliation that overwhelmed her. He wanted to say something; he tried twice and could only manage: "You know, it's not the end of the world!"

She wouldn't look at him. Her body shook in a convulsion of grief, as though his words had touched it off. He tried again. "Remember, your pa's an old man, Eve — and he's scared by what he's seen happening to the Warbonnet. Arch Casement came along, talked big and sure of himself. I guess you might say Owen sort of let him take over his thinking. . . ."

The girl lifted her head then and looked at him through the drift of falling snowflakes, that clung to her hair and lashes and her flushed cheeks. She said dully, "You can apologize for him? You, of all people — the one that he's hurt the very most!"

He could only shake his head. There was nothing worth saying, in this blackest of moments when she saw all she had believed in crashing about her.

He turned as loose rubble spurted under bootleather, and Luke Frazee came diving into cover of the log beside him. Frazee had lost his hat; despite the cold, his broken face was streaming with sweat. He clutched a smoking gun in one hand, grabbed Martin's hurt arm with the other in a grip that made him wince and jerk free. "Damn it!" the man cried hoarsely. "This is your doing — making Tom and them others think they'd stand by while we tried your crazy notion! Well, how are you going to get us out?"

"I don't know," he said honestly.

"We could try to swim the river. Some might even make it — but with most of us it'd be like shooting fish in a barrel, for those guns on the rim. I figure there's just one thing in our favor." The single, gleaming eye shifted, moving slightly beyond him.

"We got a hostage. Maybe we can buy our way."

Martin didn't have to look to know the direction of the man's stare, or the run of his twisted thoughts. He said coldly, "She's not a hostage."

"Far as I'm concerned, she is! And if they hope to see her alive —"

The muzzle of Frazee's gun was turning full on Eve St. Clair's unsuspecting back when Martin knocked it aside, with the hard edge of his palm. "Cut it out!" he said, in a fierce whisper. "I know how you feel about St. Clair; I know what he did to you. But you're not taking it out on his girl! You're not even going to suggest it!"

The man scowled, his ruined face ugly with temper. The breath hissed explosively from his lips. But he couldn't meet the other's challenging stare. He broke gaze, turning away from it.

And then Arch Casement's voice sounded into a lull in the shooting; Martin heard the unmistakable note of triumph. "All right, you down there! Listen, and listen close! We just took a look into one of your supply wagons, and I guess you know what we found. Almost a case of dynamite — caps and fuses and everything we need." He paused for the effect; Ed Martin, appalled, felt a kind of sick sensation, as though his interior organs had hardened and turned slowly over within him.

"So, let's put an end to this foolishness! I want to see every man of you on his way up here, with his hands above his head. And don't wait until I lose patience!"

Luke Frazee's horrified protest stuck in his throat; his blinded face twisted with such a look that Martin thought he could almost smell the terror. "They wouldn't! Oh God, no! They wouldn't use dynamite on us?"

"Of course not. They wouldn't dare," Martin answered scornfully — and with a surety he wished he really felt. Then he forgot the other completely as a sound he heard brought him around.

"Eve!" he exclaimed.

He reached for her but it was too late; she had already left her place behind the log. She had scrambled over it and stood directly in the open, where any hasty bullet could have found her. She had her hands pressed together at her breast, her head tilted far back as she stared upward into the snowfall spiraling past the rim. "Eve!" Martin called again, hoarsely. *"Get down!"*

She ignored him. "Pa!" she cried. "Pa, can you hear me?"

No answer at all, for a moment. Then the

voice of St. Clair came across the stillness, holding a note of shock. "Evie? That ain't you down there?" Careless of danger, the old man moved forward until the whole gaunt shape of him was silhouetted plainly. "Where are you? Let me see you!"

"You've got to stop this, Pa — you've got to stop it *now!*" Suddenly she was starting to climb, and already having trouble as her boots slipped on loose rubble and snow.

Martin, watching in indecision, heard the whistle of breath through Luke Frazee's set teeth; he turned to look and there was Frazee with his arm steadied against the top of the rotting log, hand gun drawing a careful bead on the old man who stood exposed up there on the rim. Martin saw the eager keenness in the broken face. Then he managed to get hold of the man's gunwrist and slammed it against the wood, had to do it twice before pain forced the fingers to open and let the weapon fall.

Frazee pulled away, clutching the bruised hand and savagely cursing him; but he didn't even hear.

He was turning back to watch the girl try to climb that slope and reach her father; though the guns had been startled into silence they could begin again at any moment — tightened nerves could work a trigger by accident, just as fatally as by design. With the thought, fear for her safety made sweat break across his ribs, despite the numbing cold.

When he saw her stumble and go to her knees, a small slide starting, it decided him. Setting a hand against the log he vaulted over and went sprinting after her, his six-gun swinging to his stride. He reached the girl and put a grip on her arm to lift and steady her; she shot him a single blind, unseeing look. After that they were both climbing the steep trail, with the rim just above them now and Owen St. Clair tense and waiting.

The rim was broken and weathered, giving excellent cover to those who attacked the canyon below. Just where the trail broke over, a dead snag of a pine tree jutted; and here Martin whirled and set his back against the trunk, his gun leveled — he expected a bullet, but none came. His hasty glance found them all — Casement's men, and St. Clair's, in protected positions along the edge of the dropoff with six-shooters and rifles ready at any moment to resume the fighting; from Rafter 9 he saw Whitey Lewis and Gentry and others he had spotted as Casement's hired guns, but — as Sheridan had predicted — none of the cowhands who'd made up the old Tuthill crew. So far as he could see there was not much sign of effective shooting from the depths of the canyon. He noticed one man who sat propped against a tree trunk nursing a smashed and bleeding shoulder, and felt no particular compassion when he recognized St. Clair's puncher with the too-ready fists, Harry Doyle.

But no one gave Ed Martin any notice at all, just then. They were all watching Eve St. Clair, who had hurried directly to her father and stood before him now, eyes searching his face. Her voice when she spoke was almost a whisper, trembling with hurt. "Oh, Pa! How could you? In the name of all that's decent!" She glanced down, saw the gun in his hand. When she snatched it from him and flung it away he made no effort to prevent her; to Martin the old man seemed incredibly changed — his face gray, the cheek muscles loosened by shock.

"Answer me!" Eve seized her father's arm in both her hands, as though she would shake the truth out of him. "Was everyone else right about you — telling me things I wouldn't let myself believe?" She flung a flashing, angry stare at Arch Casement, who stood motionless beside a pried-open wooden box with a stick of yellow dynamite forgotten in one hand. "It was *your* doing, wasn't it? My pa would never have taken part in such a thing if you hadn't come along, corrupting him and fooling us all. . . ."

"You don't understand," old St. Clair said heavily. "Don't blame this on Arch Casement. It's a stinkin' world, that takes an old man's son from him — and then sends a drought to tear down everything he spent a lifetime building. But, nobody's breaking Chain Link! I've taken a vow to that, no matter who I have to destroy. I've got to hold it so I can have something to pass on to you — because you're all I have left, now that Hal's gone. And because I love you!"

"You're the one that doesn't understand!" she insisted, shaking her head. "You should know you'll always have my love. But I'd rather lose Chain Link a dozen times over, than have to lose my respect for you!" She flung out a hand toward the members of his crew, who were listening with expressionless faces. "Look at these men, Pa. Do you think they *like* what you're making them do? Yet they'll never tell you — they've taken your orders too long. So *I* have to do it!

"I'm telling you, Pa! Send them home. Call this whole thing off — or you'll lose me for good!"

No one had ever given Owen St. Clair an ultimatum. Slowly the old man turned his head. He ran his glance across the faces of his riders, seeming really to see the disapproval there for the first time. He lifted a hand and passed it across his mouth and let it fall as though it were a heavy weight. His shoulders lost their stiffness. "I guess you really mean it," he said tonelessly. And to his crew: "Go on. Go home. The lot of you — get on back to the ranch!"

A roar of fury broke from Arch Casement. "No, by God! Not when we've got it almost won!" He tossed the stick of powder back into the box and started toward the St. Clairs. Owen merely flicked him with a tired glance, and turned again to his men. "You've got your orders. Fetch up the horses."

Casement saw his defeat. His chest swelled; he looked at Eve and his face was contorted, his lips drawn back. "You little bitch!" he said in a hoarse whisper. Suddenly one big hand swept around, a staggering blow that would have knocked her from her feet had Ed Martin not got to him at the same instant.

Ignoring the pain of his arm Martin grabbed Casement and pulled him off balance, taking the steam out of the blow. He flung his right fist at the man's jaw, entirely forgetting that that hand had a gun in it. The barrel of the weapon struck Casement along the side of his head, the front sight ripped a shallow furrow down his cheek. Stunned, he went to his knees.

Martin had not forgotten Whitey Lewis and the Rafter 9 gunmen. He laid a hard grip on Casement's shoulder, set the muzzle of his gun to Casement's temple and threw a warning that stopped them before they could go into action: "Make a mistake, and Casement pays for it!"

The towhead glared at him, his own drawn gun a heavy threat. He said, "Let him go, mister!"

"Maybe you can kill me," Martin answered. "But if you do, Casement won't live for you to collect your hire!" With his thumb he pulled the hammer back to full cock.

The sound of it at his ear, the cold pressure of the gunmuzzle, seemed to shock through the dazed numbness of the blow Casement had taken. A spasm of terror shook him. "He means it!" he cried hoarsely. "The damn fool will have us both killed before he gives ground!"

"That's using your head," Martin said, his grip firm on the man's shoulder. "Now tell them to put away their guns. Tell them to get on their horses and ride out of here."

The iron in Casement had given way completely, now. A shine of sweat mingled with the blood on his cheek; his mouth shook. He told his men, hoarsely, "Do as he says. Damn you, move!"

For a moment it was touch and go just what they would do. Martin had the feeling that these were men too proud to back willingly away from a standoff; but as they looked at their employer, on his knees in the trampled snow, and saw the corrosion of fear at work, Martin could sense the beginning of contempt. A cold look passed among them. Then, with the slightest of shrugs, Whitey Lewis shoved his six-gun into its holster and the lot of them turned, as a man, and started for the place where they had left their saddled horses.

Wary of a trick, Martin kept his gun in his hand and Casement on his knees while they mounted. Snow and mud gouted under shod hoofs as the horses were spurred into a start, and he watched them ride and disappear into the dark timber. He swung his glance, then, just in time to see the last of the Chain Link riders bearing off in another direction, taking their wounded with them. As quickly as that, it was over. The sounds of the horses died and the four of them — he and Casement and the St. Clairs — were left there alone, on the rocky lip of the gorge.

Ed Martin eased his cramped lungs, in a long outward breath. The ache of taut muscles across his shoulders was nearly unbearable. There was a gun in Casement's holster. He snaked it out, dropped it into a pocket of his coat, and let his Remington off cock but didn't holster it. With a nudge at Casement's shoulder he said gruffly, "On your feet."

The big man slowly hauled himself up. He ran a palm across his cheek, looked at the blood as though he had never seen any before.

By now, men were pouring up out of the canyon, wearing the incredulous look of those who couldn't quite believe the fight was over and victory was won. Tom Sheridan, gun still smoking, peered about him as though half looking for hidden enemies. He stared at Martin, shook his grizzled head. "I'll never know how you brought it off. . . ."

"I didn't. It's Owen and the girl you have to thank. And Casement, I suppose — for finally overplaying his hand."

Sheridan walked over to the St. Clairs, looked at the old man for a long moment. He offered his hand, then, but the other gave no evidence of seeing it. Tom Sheridan shrugged and let the hand drop.

"All right," he said. "Maybe you're not ready to go that far yet. But I've known you a long time, Owen; I'm sorry for any differences we've had, and I'm more than ready to bury the hatchet. It's for you to say."

The old rancher's piercing blue stare lifted, and he looked like a beaten man. Sagging cheeks stirred, the gray lips moved and then speech came. "I ain't changed my mind about the fence," St. Clair said bluntly. "It stays up. It was built to protect Chain Link grass and I'll fight any man that tries to take it down!" But then, as a taut stillness settled upon his hearers, his expression altered. He looked at his daughter as he added, "But the fence has a couple of gates in it. Any of you that wants to use the crossing — go ahead; I reckon I won't try to stop you."

"Thanks, Pa!" Eve said quietly.

St. Clair made a small gesture. "Maybe this snow's a good sign. Maybe we'll have a break this winter, and Warbonnet range will come back."

Tom Sheridan nodded. "I'll give you an 'amen' to that, Owen!" He turned, then, to the others. "You heard what he said. We won our point here; the crossings are open. Snow could be letting up some. We all got cattle to move!"

That was the signal for a general burst of activity. In very short order, horses were saddled, the wagons reloaded and hitched. A couple of men who had been hurt in the fighting had been helped up out of the canyon; these were loaded into the wagon beds and the teams got the wagons rolling. Tom Sheridan, plainly anxious to be gone, reined in his restless horse for a moment in front of Ed Martin.

"I guess you know we appreciate what you did. If we can help in any way to finish your own job here, you'll let us know?"

"Sure."

"Will you be riding into town now?"

"Not just yet," Martin told him. "I sent Charlie Runyon to fetch the sheriff out here. I guess I'll have to wait for them."

Sheridan looked over at the St. Clairs. "How about you folks? Would you like me to ride with you, make sure you get home? Owen doesn't look so good."

Eve smiled her thanks, but shook her head. "You're anxious to get going; you've got a lot to do and we wouldn't want to hold you back. We'll be all right."

"Whatever you say." He nodded and touched hat brim to her. A moment later

Tom Sheridan was spurring away, hard, to overtake his riders.

Afterward, Martin watched Owen St. Clair pull himself stuffly into the saddle, ready to offer a hand but suspecting that the old man would refuse his help. Like Sheridan, he was worried. Owen had an odd manner and an odd look; he had not rallied from his defeat, to anything like his normal arrogant vigor. Eve saw Martin's concern, and she leaned a little from the saddle to tell him, quietly, "He'll be all right. I've never seen him quite like this — but, then, he's taken a beating today. He's made concessions that didn't come easy to a man of his pride. And I hurt him, badly. But if I can just be alone with him a while. . . ."

He nodded. "I wish I could help. I'm sorry, Eve. Truly sorry — for everything."

He meant, for the destruction of the image she might have had of Arch Casement — the brutal blow of Casement's hand across her face that had ended whatever there had been between them. He wasn't sure if she would understand. But he knew she did when she looked at him for a moment and then said soberly, "I have no regrets, Ed. None at all. . . ."

He stood a long time looking after them when they had vanished into the trees.

Chapter Fifteen

The snow had nearly stopped, for the time at least. Only an occasional flake drifted down to join the white ground covering; the clouds lay leadenly overhead and the cold had settled on this mountain country, congealing a man's breath and creeping insidiously into his limbs. Ed Martin stamped his feet and swung his arms, feeling the hurt of the torn tissues, the general drained weariness. Then he walked over to throw a couple of sticks into the fire.

Arch Casement, seated on a stump with hands spread to the warmth, made no move of head or body; but his eyes, peering through lowered brows, followed the other's motions as Martin proceeded to build a cigarette from materials he took from his shirt pocket. The lawman offered the makings and, when Casement shook his head, put them away again and proceeded to light his smoke with a burning splinter plucked from the fire.

Casement said finally, "Well, what do you think you've got in mind for me?" When the lawman merely looked at him, the prisoner's mouth hardened in anger. "If you know when you're smart, friend, you'll look the other way while I get my horse, yonder, and ride out of here!"

"Oh?"

"You got no case against me," the man retorted, clipping the words. "Maybe you're thinking you do, because of what happened down there in the canyon? That was hardly anything more than a misunderstanding. Perhaps a few threats were made — but nobody was even seriously hurt. The courts in this state are too busy to even listen to any charge you could make out of it."

This made sense and Martin had to admit it, though he showed nothing in his expressionless face. He said calmly, "There might be other things. I was thinking I'd check the file in the marshal's office in Denver."

"You wouldn't find me in it," Casement answered at once, with such perfect confidence that Martin was inclined to believe him. "I've kept my skirts clean; there's nothing anyone can pin on me. If you want to find that out the hard way, go right ahead."

Martin dragged at the cigarette, letting the man guess at the run of his thoughts. "I'll tell you what," he said finally. "I've only about half finished the job I was sent here to do. Help me lick the other half and we might do business."

"Just how do you mean?" the other demanded, his eyes turning cautious.

"Get me Mort Browder."

"What makes you think I — ?" Casement started to say indignantly. But then his manner changed. The eyes narrowed; a half smile quirked his mouth. "Oh. So you did see us from the ridge, this morning!"

Martin nodded. "I figured he was reporting the mess he made, trying to pick me off at my campfire — that would have been on your orders, naturally. If I'd had a rifle with me, I could have taken care of him right then; but I didn't, and so the job's still to finish. Well, what about it?"

Arch Casement came slowly to his feet. "I give you Browder, and you let me ride free — is that it?" He shrugged. "Sure, I'd make a deal like that — except, I don't know a damn thing to tell you! Who can say where to look for a maniac like Browder? Or when? He fades out of nowhere and he's gone the same way. For all you know he could be watching us both, this very minute! But if he doesn't want us to know, we damn well won't." And Casement actually turned and put a nervous look around him, as though he were hunting for the killer in this black-and-white world that lay about them.

Martin resisted a queasy impulse to search the timber, himself. Meditatively drawing at his smoke, he held his eyes on the other man. "Just what has he got on you, Casement?"

That earned him a keen stab from Casement's truculent glance. "You're guessing! Supposing there was anything — do you think you could hurt me with it now, any worse than I have been already? On the word of a man like that?" He shook his head emphatically. "I've said it all; the rest is up to you. You can waste your time taking me in and trying to book me — or, you can give me back my gun and turn me loose. Make up your mind!"

Martin studied him, testing the strengths and the weaknesses in this man, probing behind the facade of bluster to the hollow core he had discovered within. He took the cigarette from his lips, looked at it, flung it angrily into the fire. With a jerk of his head he said, "I'll keep the gun. Your horse is yonder. Take him and get out of my sight!"

Alone, he found himself a victim of irritable moods that held him rooted still before the fire — boneweary, nursing his stiffening arm and wondering where he turned next. He could feel satisfaction over as much of the job as had been accomplished; but while Mort Browder ran free, there was the nagging need to be taking some action — even if he didn't know what it should be. Afternoon was dragging on to an early dusk. He shook off his lethargy, kicked out what was left of the fire, and went to mount the dun. And as he was checking the cinch he heard a sound that brought him up and sent his hand to his gun.

His first thought was of Browder; but the rider who came toward him, as he waited cautiously beside his horse, was Charlie Runyon. The old puncher wore a peevish scowl. He pulled rein and hitched over in the saddle, to look down at him.

"That was sure a wild goose chase you sent me on!"

"Adamson wouldn't come?"

"I never even saw him. He's gone — cleaned out. His badge was on the desk with his resignation pinned to it."

Martin thought this over. "So the job finally looked too much for him — just when somebody else was getting it straightened out. Too bad." He shrugged. "Or, maybe it's just as well. Warbonnet deserves a sheriff with a little more spine to him. Now you'll have a chance to pick one."

"That's what I figure," the other said. "I ran into some of the boys from Chain Link, and from what they told me it sounds like I missed out on *all* the fun." He looked around. "Where's Casement?"

"Gone," Martin answered, and explained as he saw the other's quick frown, "No, I didn't much like turning him loose, either, but without a specific charge I could see no use in holding him. After all, there's not much damage he can do now — he played a bluff, and when he lost St. Clair he lost the whole game.

"It's Mort Browder I'm concerned about. He's not a man who takes defeat — he has to take it out on somebody, or something. Last night he didn't manage to put a bullet into me, so he murdered my bronc. I don't like to think what he might do now."

Charlie Runyon nodded slowly, scowling. "I see your problem." He rubbed his leathery jaw, as he watched Ed Martin jerk the latigo tight, then turn the stirrup and pull himself into the leather. "You got any plans for stopping him?"

He shook his head tiredly. "All I know is that that madman is somewhere here on the Warbonnet — in a killing mood, as like as not, knowing that the man he was backing has lost the fight. . . ."

"Not to change the subject," the old puncher said suddenly, interrupting, "Where's Owen? And the girl?"

Martin stared at him a moment. "Why, they went home. I thought you said you ran into them?"

"Not them — it was some of the boys. They told me Evie and her pa stayed behind. With you."

"No, they left — it must have been half an hour ago. Seems strange you wouldn't have passed them somewhere. . . ." Suddenly the two men were sharing a look that revealed the first stirring of alarm they both felt.

"Say it!" Charlie Runyon exclaimed in a hushed voice. "You're thinking about Browder!"

"Partly. I'm also thinking that Owen wasn't looking good. He appeared a sick man, to me. Like what he went through here might have been too much for him, at last. I wouldn't want to think of him being taken bad, with them alone on the trail in this weather."

The puncher's face took on a sober cast. "You know, it could be even more serious than you think, Ed. Evie doesn't know, but the old man's heart ain't good. A fact!" Charlie said, nodding, as he caught Martin's quick stare. "He always seemed tough as they come. Still and all, the doctor told us the truth, months ago; only, Owen swore us both to secrecy — didn't want his girl worrying. I been thinking that was maybe more'n half the reason he went hogwild, like he did, backing Casement. He didn't know how much time he might have left, and he wanted things settled, when he did have to go."

Martin swore softly. "God, I wish I'd known this! I'd never have let them start back to Chain Link, with Owen looking the way he did."

"Yeah. . . ."

Suddenly, without more words, they were both touching steel to their horses.

The snow that had slackened during the past hour was beginning again, and a wind was rising out of the north, rocking tall pineheads against a dark sky. The tracks of the St. Clair horses were plain enough, a double line of them in the unbroken snowfield, leading away from the river gorge.

It was beyond the first scatter of timber that they found the sign that told what had happened. They pulled up, a growing sense of disaster welling in them both.

"He was waiting under that pine," Ed Martin said, pointing to the scuffing of snow beneath it. "They saw him and tried to turn back but he got between to head them off. There wasn't any shooting. He must have known I'd hear it; and I remember, now, neither Eve nor her father had a gun. So they had to give ground, and he drove them straight ahead of him — right where he wanted them to go. Straight up into the hills!" Martin pointed to where the confused sign of three ridden horses, the prints overlapping, led off into a brush-choked gully that opened into the first timbered rises dead ahead of them.

Charlie Runyon raised a hand and scrubbed it across his face, pulling his mouth out of shape; the hand was trembling slightly. "You figure — Browder?"

Martin's face was bleak. He lifted the reins, saying only, "I figure we could have lost too much time, already!"

Feeling a touch of panic that he tried to force under control, he kicked the dun ahead into the blind whiteness sweeping out of the timber. He thought it must surely be too late.

Arch Casement came flagging into the Rafter 9 yard on the spur, the flanks of his mount running red from the cruel roweling it had taken. When he saw activity about the buildings, a quick curiosity bested the savage mood that had ridden him all the way from Rocky Point; he curbed the wild-eyed bronc and sat a moment, glowering in puzzlement.

The yard seemed filled with horses, tied to hitch posts and corral railings, all under saddles and blanket rolls; as he watched, Whitey Lewis came from the bunkhouse with a pair of saddle bags across his shoulder. He walked to where his bay gelding was tied, slung the bags in place behind the cantle and began to lash them down. And then he looked up, his hands going motionless, as Casement kicked his tired horse forward across the hooftramped mud of the yard.

"Where do you think you're going?" Casement demanded, his voice loud with angry suspicion.

"I'm going," the towheaded man replied. "That's all you have to know."

"Quitting me? Is that it?" Casement's thick chest swelled as he fought to sort out the furious words that crowded his tongue. And then he paused, the words still unspoken, as he saw the other men.

He turned his head slowly, seeing them waiting by their horses, moving up from the barn and bunkshack and corral. Some carried gear, or saddle rolls; one had a rifle in a scabbard under his arm. They all wore a definite look of men in the process of packing up, moving on; and rage shook him as he saw beyond any doubt what it implied.

"So you're *all* quitting!" he said tightly. "Running at the sign of a little trouble. Hell, I knew those saddle-tramps George Tuthill handed on to me would back out if it came to a fight; but, what's got into the rest of you? Damn you, you were *paid* to fight! You're supposed to be *men!*"

"And what were *you* supposed to be?" Whitey flung back at him. His eyes behind their pale lashes held such contempt that Casement could feel the tide of warmth begin to flow up into his face. "We saw enough, Casement! One look at a man groveling on his knees tells as much as a library. We all got pay coming. We'll take it now. It's the only thing we want out of you."

Casement tried, as always at such a moment, to fall back upon bluster. "You'll get your pay when I say you've earned it!" But when he saw the iron in the looks that met his own, the bluster died. His chest felt suddenly cramped. He leaned forward, his hands upon the saddlehorn; in horror he heard the note of pleading creep into his voice, yet could not stop himself.

"Sure, we had a bad break today; but what's the loss if St. Clair did walk out on us? We don't need him! You saw how it was

— his men wouldn't even back him. We can take those river crossings right from under his nose, and hold them."

"Against the whole valley? And that marshal?" The blond gunman calmly shook his head. "No, thanks. That's not my idea of odds."

Casement felt a suspicious stinging behind his eyes. He blinked and slammed a fist on his saddlehorn in an attempt to keep back the unmanly tears of frustration. "Damn it, I tell you, there's enough of us! Even without Chain Link!"

"There's enough of *us,* maybe," Whitey said. "We're beginning to doubt that there's enough of *you!*"

And then, from the bunkhouse doorway where he stood leaning his bandaged body, Bud Flint spoke in a tone of weary impatience. "Shut up, Casement, and pay us off. Can't you see when you're licked?"

That stopped him. For a long moment he looked at Flint, knowing Flint was the final spokesman. If Bill Hammer had still been alive, he would have held the rest in line. Or — would he? Would Bill have turned his back on him, too?

It didn't matter. Hammer was dead; Rafter 9 was dead. He lifted his shoulders, feeling the iron bands tightening about his chest. He said, heavily, "Wait here." And picking up the reins, he turned his horse and rode slowly across the muddy yard to the house.

In the privacy of his office, he closed the door and stood against it a moment, aware of the sudden trembling of his whole body. By God, no! he thought, in furious rebellion. He looked at the squat iron safe in the corner behind the desk, thought of the strongbox it contained and the few hundred dollars that was all he had left of the cash he'd brought with him to the Warbonnet. The men waiting outside didn't know it, but there wasn't enough in that box to settle what he owed them. . . . His eyes narrowed. The hell with them, then!

He wasn't going to be left alone to face the enemies he had made here — left with a ranch he couldn't hope to run without crew and foreman, leases he could never afford to renew, a beef herd that had been stripped to pay for a damned barb wire fence that was no longer of any use to him. Flint and those other bastards out there could whistle for their pay! While they were whistling, he would take the money and be out of here before they knew he was gone.

It was risky, of course — they'd have his hide if they caught him. He crossed to the desk, opened a drawer and took out an extra gun he always kept there; he spun the cylinder, checked the loads, and felt better as he dropped it into his holster. After that he was on his heels in front of the safe, working the combination. He pulled open the door, brought out the tin strongbox which was all it held except for papers that were less than worthless to him now. His hand closed on crisp green bills; in the long run, he saw with sudden clarity, a man was a fool to put his faith in anything else but hard cash — cash that could be folded and put into a pocket, cash that you could take with you when a game went against you and you found yourself on the run again. It was a lesson he had learned in his earliest, fiddlefooted beginnings; it was one he had been a fool ever to let himself forget —

The voice behind him said, "Put that money back in the box. And send it over here toward me."

There had been no sound at all, not even the opening of the door. He gasped and came around so fast that his legs tangled and he went down in a sprawl; from where he lay, the narrow shape of the man in the doorway seemed to reach on, up and up, toward the very ceiling. Casement looked at him and couldn't force speech from a throat that was suddenly squeezed tight.

Mort Browder said, "I told you I'd be watching to see how you played this hand you'd dealt yourself. You played it like a damned greenhorn!"

He found his voice, or something that sounded vaguely like it. "You can't blame it all on me! Blame St. Clair, for backing out. Blame that marshal you promised to get rid of. . . ."

"Martin. . . ." The narrow head wagged slowly. The pale eyes shone. "No, I haven't settled with him, yet. But that's all right — our trails will cross, another time. Just now I'm more interested in getting out of this damned Warbonnet country before the storm has time to clog the passes. And, I'm not going emptyhanded." He put out a hand, waggled the fingers. "The box!" he said again.

"No!"

Turned desperate and reckless at thought of finding himself suddenly penniless — precisely where he had started out, ten years before — Arch Casement dropped the box and made a hopeless effort to reach the gun in his holster. He had not even got a hand on it when Browder's bullet took him squarely in the face.

It drove him back against the safe door,

his lifeless weight slamming it shut; that sound mingled with the deafening concussion of the shot, and then, somewhere out in the ranch yard, there were the first questioning shouts. Moving without haste, Mort Browder paced forward and stooped for the strongbox, scooped out the packet of bills. He looked them over, stuffed them into a pocket. He was turning away when, as though on an afterthought, he paused, looked again at the man he had killed. One dead hand lay limply open, the fingers slightly curled. With a faint smile tilting his narrow mouth, Mort Browder rocked the cylinder of his gun, shook out the still-smoking shell, and dropped it carefully into Casement's lifeless palm.

After that, with the nearing sounds in the yard to prod him, he crossed the room again in a couple of effortless strides. He was turning toward the rear of the house as the men outside hit the front veranda, in an excited, yelling rush.

Chapter Sixteen

It was Ed Martin who discovered the body, lying half covered already by the rapidly drifting snow. His first move was to draw the Remington and fire three spaced shots, the signal he and Charlie Runyon had agreed upon. Only afterward did he dismount, his cold body moving stiffly. He got the reins of the riderless horse, that had snagged in a tangle of brush. He was holding it, together with his own animal, when Charlie came floundering up through the drifts shouting, "You find something?"

Martin nodded at the body. Charlie cursed in surprise and swung down. He leaned to touch the stiffening shoulder and, as he did, Luke Frazee's head rolled limply and grotesquely. "Neck's broken," Martin said. "I'd say the horse fell with him — and the horse was the only thing that got up again."

"Luke Frazee!" The old puncher said the name in a tone of bewilderment. "Then, it wasn't Browder at all. . . ."

The other shook his head, looking sombrely at the dead, battered face and its single sightless eye. "I guess none of us realized just how much he really hated St. Clair, for what that beating did to him. I guess, on that one count, he was as crazy as Mort Browder. Then today he saw the war was being called off — and when he got a chance at them, alone, it was more than he could pass up."

Charlie Runyon lifted his head and peered

anxiously about him. There was little enough to see. The timber rises pressed close about them, shrouded with mist and with a tumultuous fury of wind and snow that brought the threat of early dusk upon these hills. "Where do you suppose they are, in the midst of all this?"

"I don't know." Martin's face was bleak. Wind had blown the tracks, and fresh snow had filled them, so that for the past hour he and Charlie had been searching without the help of any sign at all. "We could have ridden right over them and not known it — but we've got to believe that isn't true. We've got to assume they made it this far."

"And, from here?"

"Maybe they're running blind," Martin said. "But if they aren't, and if they don't realize they've lost him, there's only two ways they can go: Straight ahead, they reach the pass eventually; no shelter for them there. The other chance is Gold Camp, and Riley's place."

The old puncher shook his head, gloomily. "That's a long ride."

"I know. But it's their only real hope — they'd never survive a night in this weather, not if Owen's in as bad shape as you tell me. I'm betting they have sense enough to know that."

"Only one way to find out," Charlie Runyon said. "That's for us to split up. If you want to take the long chance and head for Gold Camp, then I'll go on toward the pass. And hope to God one of us finds them!"

Martin hesitated, then nodded his agreement. "I think you're right. It's the sensible thing to do. Only — be careful. Don't go taking any risks."

The old puncher snorted. "Worry about your own self! I figure I'm in considerably better condition than *you* are, right now. How's that arm?"

He flexed it stiffly; actually he was so thoroughly chilled by the raw, pummeling wind that there seemed little feeling in the arm at all. "It'll do. . . ."

Before they split up, they got Frazee's body out of the snow and across his saddle, where they lashed him on with his own catch rope. Martin tied the trailing reins over the pommel, and a slap on the rump got the animal started; with the wind at its tail it would probably keep going under its burden until it reached the flats and, eventually, its own corral. Then, they mounted and with no more ceremony than a brief "Be seeing you!" they set out on their separate ways, in search of the missing man and girl.

■ ■ ■ ■

The wretched day died in fury, the wind screaming at an ever higher pitch while light gradually leaked away out of the sky. Blown and buffeted until it seemed impossible to cling for much longer to a horse's back, Eve St. Clair could only bow her head to the storm and endure. It had been a nightmare, from the moment when they found Luke Frazee waiting to block their path and turn them back — a Luke Frazee who became a voice following them through the smother of wind and snow, calling the old man's name and howling obscene threats. Presently the voice had fallen silent; but how were they to know they had really lost him?

As if all this wasn't terrifying enough, she had then become aware of an alarming change in her father. She could never remember seeing him ill for as much as a day, except for one brief and mysterious period a year ago that had been glossed over and almost forgotten; so she thought at first it was only weariness that made him sag helplessly over the hands he clamped on the pommel of his saddle. But when she saw him sway and begin to slide sidewards out of it, she cried out and forced her mount alongside his while she put an anxious grip on his snow-encrusted sleeve to steady him. When she saw the face that he lifted, as though with terrible effort, she thought her heart had stopped.

His words came feebly, under the roar of the wind: "I'm played out. I got to rest. . . ."

"Pa! You're sick!"

"No, no! I'll be all right, I just got to rest."

But there was no hope of doing that, in this howling storm; if he got out of the saddle, Eve knew she would never get him back into it. She had been casting ahead and, in these circumstances, saw only one solution. But this storm had her confused as to place and direction; and even when she managed to rouse her father, the answers he was able to give her anxious questions were frighteningly vague. She knew it was squarely up to her — and that she had little more than guesswork to go on.

As they rode she watched the old man carefully, and she saw his weakness growing. Finally, for a safety measure, she had to dismount while she used his own saddle rope to tie his ankles together, running the line beneath the horses's belly. Her fingers, working at the knots, were stiff and nearly useless; her feet felt as lifeless as stumps. A little lightheaded, now, she began to wonder at the grotesque shapes they must make — the two of them plastered white with the snow, from hats to boots. And then her fears increased, her deepening certainty that they must be hopelessly lost.

. . . Suddenly, unbelievably, she heard a sound that could only be a door swinging and slamming in the wind. Moments later the wind itself dropped away as it was deflected by shouldering walls; the snow smother cleared enough to show her black and lightless shapes of buildings, ghosting by in the gloom. And then she saw a light, a dim trace of a lamplit window.

The horses seemed to know what it meant, for they drifted forward and came to a halt of their own accord, their heads drooping before a veranda railing. Eve raised her voice, hoping it would carry. She called twice, gave it up and was painfully dragging herself out of the saddle when the door swung open and a man and a woman came out upon the porch. The man carried a lamp which he raised high as he peered at the horses and their riders, saying, "Who'd be traveling on a night like — ?" He broke off as the light of the lamp touched Owen St. Clair's face. Eve heard his exclamation of surprise.

"Please!" she cried in a voice that sounded

to her like nothing human. "Help us. . . ."

But he stood unmoving, staring at the face of the old man in the saddle, until the woman prodded him. "Come on, now, Riley! Forget what you're thinking. They're asking our help — I reckon we can afford to give it to them. Looks to me like St. Clair needs a bed. You bring him in and get him upstairs while I'm fixing it."

Nothing was very clear, after that. Eve knew she was inside; the storm was shut away, her half-frozen body enduring the pleasant agony of thawing out. Some time later, without being sure just how much time had past, she found herself seated on the edge of a bed as she watched her father's sleeping face and saw how waxen and pale it looked, and somehow sunken in upon itself. Before he slept he had clutched her hand, while she leaned to hear him say in the faintest of murmurs, "I'm sorry. Sorry. . . ." Now the hard, veined hand was lax and limp in her own; but at least his breathing was deep and natural. Eve let herself begin to think he would be all right.

She was wearing dry clothes and a wrapper that had been given her; now the woman — Hazel Riley, she said her name was — came in with a tray of food. And Eve let herself be placed in a chair beside a crackling stove, with the tray across her knees. She looked up into the hard face of the woman; she looked around at the drab room, with its shabby furnishings and stained wallpaper and its smell of decay; and she said in deep sincerity, "You and your husband are very good to us, Mrs. Riley."

"Yeah, I kind of think we are," the woman answered bluntly, standing back to look at her with workroughened hands hugging her elbows. "After the way your old man has treated us, the past dozen years!" She indicated the food. "You gonna eat that? Now that I've gone to the trouble fixing it?"

Eve obediently started to work at it, and instantly discovered how really starved she was.

She waited until she had finished, and the tray had been take away from her and set on a rickety table, before she asked the question that had been growing in her mind: "Mrs. Riley, I'm wondering if you'll tell me what — what really happened that night my brother was killed."

She saw the woman's back stiffen. Hazel Riley turned, then, and leaned her hips against the edge of the table. "You don't really want to go through that again!"

"But I do! I want to know the truth —

from someone who was there."

After a moment, the woman evidently decided she was sincere. She shrugged and said, "What's there to tell? It was just the way me and Riley have told it all along: A couple of guys, down in the big room, got in an argument over the turn of a card. Your brother didn't know the danger he was in, didn't move out of the way fast enough; he took a bullet that wasn't meant for him." She added, "That's all there was to it. And if your pa still thinks it was in any way Ed Martin's fault — he's crazy!"

"Oh, I never did believe *that!*" Eve said, quickly.

Too quickly, perhaps, and too emphatically. She saw the look Hazel Riley shot her, from thoughtfully narrowed eyes that seemed to think they could read more than she was saying, and next moment was angry to find herself coloring furiously. She thought to herself, you'd better let this go! And yet, she knew she couldn't; it was too important a matter, something she had to know — and this, her one chance of ever finding out. Stubbornly she asked, "But what went on before the shooting? I mean — what had they both been doing?"

The woman laughed shortly. "It was pathetic to watch! They was green as grass, the two of them. Any fool could see it must have been the first time they'd either been in a place like this."

Eve felt her fingers tighten until the nails hurt her palms. She let the slight pain steel her to the question she must ask. "I always understood you had —" She swallowed. "Girls working here, then. Did he — did either of them — ?"

"Get took upstairs?" Hazel Riley finished, with that same shrewd and probing look. "Oh, no, honey. They'd have been too scared even to think of it! Anyway, I'd never allowed it; not kids that young." She leaned forward suddenly. "Hey! Wait a minute! I get it now. Your trouble is, you're *jealous!* Well, what do you know? You been jealous of that Ed Martin fellow all these years — over something you thought might have happened, but never really did. . . ."

This time Eve didn't blush. She was too overwhelmed by the truth of what she'd just heard, to be embarrassed. She thought, in sober and shocking self knowledge: Why, it's so!

Ever since, she'd been wondering about that night, had let herself imagine all kinds of dreadful things. An insulted and deeply hurt young girl had let herself believe the boy she idolized had ridden up here to the arms of some cheap and horrible woman; and, secretly, this had been a worse thing to her than any blame he might have had in her brother's death. She saw now that she had never really forgiven him — and now it was she who cried, silently, forgive *me,* my dear! For being a prig and a blind fool!

She lifted her head, her eyes smarting from unshed tears of shame — and with a start saw a man standing by the bed looking silently down at her father.

She had heard no one at all on the creaking stairs, had heard no one enter. In the first glimpse she thought it must be the woman's husband, Riley; next instant, she realized she had never seen this tall man with the odd, narrow face. Surprise, and something strangely close to dread, went through her. Then Hazel Riley saw her expression and turned her head, and came quickly erect.

"Where did you come from?" she demanded, in a harsh voice. "How did you get in here?"

The man turned and looked from one to the other, with a pale and piercing stare — and all at once, without anyone telling her, Eve felt with a choking certainty that she knew who he was. "Two Chain Link horses in the barn," Mort Browder said softly. "St.

Clair, I'd seen before. So this must be his girl." The pale eyes found her and moved over her deliberately, in a way that made her shudder as though she had been touched by an unclean hand. It brought her stumbling to her feet, clutching the wrapper more tightly about her.

Even Hazel Riley — seemingly a woman capable of handling anything — sounded strained and frightened. "Bad night out," she said, too loudly.

The chill of the storm clung to him. He had shucked his outer coat and hat somewhere but his jeans and boots were dark with melted snow. He rubbed his hands together silently as he nodded. "I'm on my way out of this country. And it's no night to try the pass."

"You want something to eat, maybe? If you'll just come downstairs —"

He ignored the suggestion. "Who else is around?"

She answered quickly, "My husband."

"Oh, yeah. Him." It was a complete dismissal. Browder said it like a sneer, those compelling eyes not moving from Eve's white face. She felt her knees starting to turn to jelly; only an effort kept her from putting a hand against the back of the chair to steady herself.

Hazel Riley saw all this, saw what was in Browder's face, and she made a last valiant effort. She stepped in between the two, actually had the temerity to lay a hand on the killer's arm in a friendly gesture. "Let's go on downstairs," she said. "I'll see what I can find to fix for you."

"No!" He didn't raise his voice, didn't even put his stare on her; but her hand dropped hastily away. "*You* go," he said softly. "I think I'll stay here with my friends, the St. Clairs."

A despairing look passed between Eve and the Riley woman. Then the latter shook her head, with a helpless gesture. She was starting to turn toward the door when a sudden subtle change came over Mort Browder. His head lifted. What sound he had heard, above the battering of the wind about the eaves, no one else would ever know. But he drew his gun, shoving Hazel Riley roughly aside, and moved past her with that strange and silent stride of his, out onto the balcony that overlooked the big room below. He was standing like that, gunbarrel slanted across the railing, when the outside door suddenly burst open, as a gust of wind took it from the hand that had thrown the latch.

In a smother of blown snow, Ed Martin stomped inside. Light flickered in the chimney of an oil lamp on the bar, wind whooped through the cavernous room and rattled the pages of a gaudy wall calendar. He had to put his shoulder briefly to the panel, to force it closed. He looked around, seeing only an empty room.

Martin could have checked the barn in order to learn if the St. Clair horses were there; but his mind — dulled by the storm, by the ache of his wounded arm, by the fatigue of drained energy — hadn't worked that logically. He stood kicking the snow from his boots, palming his cheeks with a half-frozen hand and starting to fumble at the fastenings of the snow-encrusted canvas coat, as he lifted a call into shadowed stillness: "Riley? Anyone here?

Silence and emptiness mocked him. An inward warning told him it was useless. He had made a wrong guess, and it was too late now to do anything more about it. Now, any chance the St. Clairs had would be up to Charlie Runyon.

This dismal certainty was settling on him as he pulled off the wet and shapeless hat, that stuck to his forehead briefly and came away as a heavy wad of soaked felt. He moved over and dropped it onto a table and was standing there, uncertainly waiting, when he heard the sudden outcry and commotion break loose overhead, on the balcony at the room's far end.

Martin jerked about. The upward-angling stairs were lost in darkness; but an open door at their top gave some dim light, that limned the balcony railing — and the pair of figures struggling there. He knew the voice he heard was a woman's; incredibly, it had belonged to Eve St. Clair. Now he heard it again, breathless and shrill with terror: "Ed! Hurry — get away!"

That broke him free, and started him for the stairs with a hand pawing at the skirt of his windbreaker and trying to reach the holster. His boots hit the treads; they groaned as he went up them. He could make out the struggling pair, now — could see the man, and Eve clinging frantically to his gunwrist, and the faint gleam of metal.

But a sweep of the man's arm flung her away, so that she struck the wall and was sent heavily down to her knees. At the same moment he was whirling back to face Martin, half way up the steps. Lamplight through the door showed the unmistakable, narrow face of Mort Browder; and it showed the revolver he swung into line against the lawman.

In the same instant, Martin had got his hand on the Remington. He stopped climbing, sank down with his shoulders against the wall as chilled, stiff fingers hauled the gun out of the holster. The weapon on the landing above him exploded, even as he was lifting it. He saw the blinding smear of the muzzleflash and heard lead slap into the wall, inches from his body. He caught his breath, held it, and fired upward across the rail.

He heard it hit. Only Browder's grip on the balcony railing kept him from being driven backward off his feet. Instead, he stood there with his long frame bending slowly over the banister. His gaunt head dropped forward; the gun fell from his hand and landed with a thud on the floor of the barroom, below. And then, quite slowly, he doubled into a jackknife and went across the railing, his body turning once as it fell.

Echoes of gunfire boomed and rumbled through the big room, exactly as they had done on the night eleven years ago when Hal St. Clair died. Slowly, Ed Martin pushed to his feet.

He shoved the smoking Remington away, and went on up the stairs. In the lighted doorway, Hazel Riley stood as though transfixed, staring at him; past her, through the door, he caught a glimpse of old St. Clair lying in the bed, his eyes closed and his face nearly as colorless as the pillow under his head. But Martin gave these two scarcely a look. He went directly on to where Eve lay, stunned by Mort Browder's blow. He knelt and took her in his arms.

"Ed? You're not — ? He didn't —"

Her hands clutched at him; then her face was against his chest and he was comforting her, kissing her hair and her cheek and, at last, her mouth. "It's all right," he said, as he would sooth a child. "It's going to be all right, now." It was odd that he should feel so certain of it.

A renewed gust of wind pummeled the building like a fist, rattled windows, tumbled howling about the eaves. Down below a door slammed and Joe Riley came hurrying into the barroom, stammering startled questions that ceased abruptly as he halted to stare at Mort Browder's flung and lifeless shape.

With loving gentleness, Ed Martin lifted the trembling girl to her feet.

ABOUT THE AUTHOR

D(wight) B(ennett) Newton is the author of a number of notable Western novels. Born in Kansas City, Missouri, Newton went on to complete work for a Master's degree in history at the University of Missouri. From the time he first discovered Max Brand in Street and Smith's *Western Story Magazine,* he knew he wanted to be an author of Western fiction. He began contributing Western stories and novelettes to the Red Circle group of Western pulp magazines published by Newsstand in the late 1930s. During the Second World War, Newton served in the US Army Engineers and fell in love with the central Oregon region when stationed there. He would later become a permanent resident of that state and Oregon frequently serves as the locale for many of his finest novels. As a client of the August Lenniger Literary Agency, Newton found that every time he switched publishers he was given a different byline by his agent. This complicated his visibility. Yet in notable novels from *Range Boss* (1949), the first original novel ever published in a modern paperback edition, through his impressive list of titles for the Double D series from Doubleday, *The Oregon Rifles, Crooked River Canyon,* and *Disaster Creek* among them, he produced a very special kind of Western story. What makes it so special is the combination of characters who seem real and about whom a reader comes to care a great deal and Newton's fundamental humanity, his realization early on (perhaps because of his study of history) that little that happened in the West was ever simple but rather made desperately complicated through the conjunction of numerous opposed forces working at cross purposes. Yet, through all of the turmoil on the frontier, a basic human decency did emerge. It was this which made the American frontier experience so profoundly unique and which produced many of the remarkable human beings to be found in the world of Newton's Western fiction.

We hope you have enjoyed this Large Print book. Other Thorndike, Wheeler, and Chivers Press Large Print books are available at your library or directly from the publishers.

For information about current and upcoming titles, please call or write, without obligation, to:

Publisher
Thorndike Press
295 Kennedy Memorial Drive
Waterville, ME 04901
Tel. (800) 223-1244

or visit our Web site at:

www.gale.com/thorndike
www.gale.com/wheeler

OR

Chivers Large Print
published by BBC Audiobooks Ltd
St James House, The Square
Lower Bristol Road
Bath BA2 3SB
England
Tel. +44(0) 800 136919
email: bbcaudiobooks@bbc.co.uk
www.bbcaudiobooks.co.uk

All our Large Print titles are designed for easy reading, and all our books are made to last.